He realized their mission was—

With a roar like all God's cannon, the USS *Commodore Jones* blew up.

Samson saw it happen because, pulling at the oars, he was facing that way. Behind him, Jim Strang, pulling on the forward oars, gasped.

The little ship, smaller than a Coast Guard cutter in Samson's own time, had been working her way forward gingerly on the placid surface of the James, gently illuminated by the afternoon sun at one moment, and in the next had vanished in a great red blast.

Where she had been, water fountained up two or three stories high, and above that, high in the sun, Samson could see tumbling boards and wood....

The wave came next, a rock-hard shove against the soles of their feet through the wooden planking of the rowboat, followed by the hard buck and plunge of the boat as more waves threatened to capsize her.

John Barnes

TIMERAIDER

UNION
FIRES

A GOLD EAGLE BOOK FROM
WORLDWIDE®

TORONTO • NEW YORK • LONDON
AMSTERDAM • PARIS • SYDNEY • HAMBURG
STOCKHOLM • ATHENS • TOKYO • MILAN
MADRID • WARSAW • BUDAPEST • AUCKLAND

First edition December 1992

ISBN 0-373-63606-7

Special thanks and acknowledgment to
John Barnes for his contribution to this work.

UNION FIRES

UNION
FIRES

1

The Wind Between Time blew harsher and colder than it ever had before. Even the first time Daniel Samson could remember dying, the soul-chilling fingers of the Wind hadn't clawed into his mind with such icy, bleak, bitter force as this.

He hung in the Wind Between Time, suspended above the whole body of all of his past lives spread out before him. There were more than he could think of at one time. They seemed to stretch back in time forever. But three of them now were different. They gave off a glow, a feeling of harmony, a scent of roses—because there were no senses as ordinarily known in the Wind Between Time, he could only say how something was by comparison. But there were also no lies or falsehoods possible, and so he knew immediately not what a thing felt or looked like, but what it was.

And those three lives now were good. There was a shine, a clear bell-like sound, a sweetness to them.

But the rest, stretching into infinity, were gray and withered, or discordant, or stank.

Now that he had become increasingly able to master this other side of the grave, Samson could perceive them clearly for the first time, and he could at last feel deep in his soul how foul most of his past lives were. Those were lives that had closed as unbroken records of shame, waste, crime and betrayal.

Scant weeks before, as Samson now experienced time, there had been only one life that glowed. Since then, he had returned to a lifetime that had ended in the falling timbers of a blown-apart house in central Italy in 1944, and in the few days he had been there, he had redeemed that past life; that life, too, now glowed. Not long after that, in 1846 and 1847 he had fought and died in the mountains and deserts of New Mexico, and that life, too, was won back to the light and the harmony.

He hadn't changed a bit of history, he knew. The world was still what it had been, still what it was fated to be. But he had changed his part in it, so that what had been one more sorry blotch on humanity's record had become a small but nevertheless real and defiant anthem of triumph.

This was the right he had won in the 1990s, when he had died under the chattering AK-47 of a psychopathic gunman, defending the lives of helpless people by stopping the madman with his bare hands. He could win his past lives back to the light, one at a time, as long as he did not fail, ever. He had won two now, but he hadn't known until he looked down and out across the great sweep of past lives that there were so many.

Jeez, but the Wind Between Time was cold this time! It was so hard to think!

The enormous number of his past lives was just one of many things that he'd learned on this long voyage, but it was the first that had truly frightened him. Could he honestly win back every one of those lives without failing even once? And if he did fail, what appalling sacrifices and terrible things would he have to accomplish to pay back for his failure?

A few weeks ago, as you reckon time, a voice said in his head, *you didn't know you were in danger, and you hadn't fought or won any of these. The day you died you merely thought you were an amiable failure at life, a hero who had come home from his war only to prove incapable of living at peace.*

The voice belonged to Master Xi, whom Samson had met at his best friend Matt Perney's dojo, back in life, on the day Samson had died. Master Xi seemed to be Samson's guide for these experiences, but whether he was an angel or a sage, a living Buddha or the last of the red-hot swamis, or just part of an ongoing and amazingly detailed hallucination while Samson bled to death on a gurney, Samson didn't know.

As usual, Master Xi did have a point. There was no question that where there had been no hope at all, now there was a little bit.

For that matter, there was the other thing Master Xi was right about. Real courage was a matter of seeing exactly how much and what kind of danger you were in, and then going ahead and doing what needed to be done.

All right, then. He'd just have to get it done.

The Wind Between Time settled to its normal cold wail. It was as if the storm had turned off.

The icy, howling storm that had almost blown him away had been nothing more complicated or difficult than plain, ordinary fear.

Well, then, another lifetime to tackle and redeem. Not easy, but something he had done before and knew himself to be capable of. Which life to pick?

There was a feeling of warm laughter all around him. *You see, Daniel Samson, that once you know that the problem is fear, it no longer matters that the fear is there.*

Oh, it mattered, Samson thought, but one could face it and deal with it, and that was enough.

Now, which life to pick?

There were two things he had learned on his last trip into a past life. There, in the Mexican War, under another name, he had met a man whom he had known in World War II. Juan Bastida, or Paul Turenne, was somehow wandering down the same long, braided rope of past lives that Samson was. He knew that their paths were to cross many times, and that when they did, if Samson succeeded, their paths would cross as friends, allies and comrades in arms.

So, though he didn't know much about them yet, he apparently had friends—and perhaps enemies—who would continue from life to life. Indeed, just moments before, he had felt Bastida, or Turenne, vanish into some life that didn't happen to include Samson. It was no matter; they would meet again.

The other thing he had learned, from seeing too much of it up close, was that he absolutely hated slavery. I can't imagine I missed out on the Civil War, he thought. I'd like to be in at the kill. He looked down once more, and now he felt himself rushing swiftly downward toward one past life. All right, he thought, let's . . .

Go.

The deck was rolling under his feet, but gently, and he knew at once that he was on a river and not on the open ocean. He looked down to see what he was wearing and was momentarily flabbergasted.

He was wearing the uniform of a Confederate infantry officer.

As he looked up, he saw the Stars and Stripes floating from the stern of the little gunboat—the USS *Commodore Jones,* he realized. On the deck of what was very obviously a Union ship, he was standing around with one black slave, three other Confederates, and a red-haired teenage girl who seemed to be dressed up as Scarlett O'Hara. Just at the moment the crew was lowering a small boat into the water.

All right, Samson thought, now who the hell am I and what the hell is going on here?

Another thought struck him, and he looked again.

The red-haired girl was younger than he had ever known her in his "real" life, back in the late twentieth century, but there was no mistaking who it was: his ex-wife, Sarah, looking physically about sixteen. She was five-three, a full foot shorter than Samson, with a scattering of wide brown freckles across her snub nose and immense quantities of thick, dark, curly red hair, which was currently cleated to the top of her head by several pins. The only difference he could see was…well, maybe the corset did that, but Sarah as an adult had always been pretty flat chested, and this girl was, um, stacked.

He thought to himself, she's a kid this time around, remember that, and then another part of his mind said, and so am I.

In any case, this wouldn't exactly have been the time to make a move. He had work to do, helping to load the small boat, and she looked absolutely miserable in that flouncy, billowy white dress on this roasting, humid May day.

May 5, 1864, he realized. They were a short distance up the James River from where the Union Army of the James, under General Butler, had made landings on the little peninsula known as Bermuda Hundred, two days before.

He could hardly take his eyes off Sarah—no, that would not be her name in this life, but come to think of it, what was his?

His name was Sean Toole. He had lied about his age to get into the Army, and though he was now a first lieutenant with two years' service, he was barely seventeen.

Wait. His name was Prescott Heller. He had been a cadet at the Virginia Military Institute. When the boys of VMI had gone off to war, he had distinguished himself as one of the "Cradle Company," the elite and very young unit made up entirely of those cadets.

And now it all tumbled into place.

In this life, Daniel Samson had been a double agent. As Prescott Heller, the name he had been born under, he had gone to work for Captain Matthew Maury, CSN, at the Submarine Battery Service, which was a research-and-development branch of the Confederate Navy concerned with electrically detonating mines, but was also a major cover for a covert-operations branch. In fact, the Signal Corps, the well-known cover for the War Department Secret Service, was literally located next door to the Submarine Battery Service building at Ninth and Bank. It was much closer to the Capitol than you would have expected two apparently ''minor'' bureaus to be, but then President Davis did seem to drop in frequently. By now it was fairly well-known, and certainly understood by most Union agents, that whether you were supposedly working for General Alexander or Captain Maury, if you were assigned to service at Ninth and Bank, you were in espionage or covert operations.

That had certainly been the case with Prescott Heller. Two years ago, with forged orders and papers, he had made his way north, joined a Yankee unit at the right time and place, and as Sean Toole contrived to be brought to the attention of officers who in turn had referred him to Lafayette Baker, head of the Secret Service—the Union's equivalent to the FBI, NSA, and CIA of Samson's day.

Every Army officer in this boat was theoretically on detached service to the First District of Columbia

Cavalry, but by now it was an open secret that the First
D.C. was merely a cover for the covert-operations
branch of the Secret Service. A regiment with only
four companies, most of its men on detached service,
a majority of them officers—in Samson's own time,
any good Intelligence analyst would have had its
number instantly, and men like Maury and Alexander
were far from stupid.

Heck, allowing for time and circumstances, he
could just as easily describe it as being back in the
Special Forces. No wonder he felt at home.

And the mission was—

A hand clapped hard on his shoulder. "Friend, it's
time we got moving, and since we're plumb ranked, we
get to do the honors with the baggage."

He turned to his left. It was Matt Perney. His best
friend from his own time.

This was beginning to seem like a slightly mad family reunion.

But there was no time to think more about that, for
they were already loading bags and luggage into the
rowboat alongside the wooden gunboat. The *Jones*
and her two sister ships were inching their way up the
James, constantly alert for fire from the hostile shores,
trying to sweep the river of torpedos—the word at the
time for mines—so that Admiral Lee's ironclads could
be brought up to supply fire support for General Butler's breakout and advance.

But unlike her sister ships, the USS *Commodore
Jones* had another mission. In the confusion and
alarm spread along the roads and railroad between

Petersburg and Richmond by the sudden Union landings in force, it would be easy to—

Samson had to concentrate on getting the last of the
bags in. There seemed like a lot of it, but he recalled
from his Mexican War adventures that field equipment before the twentieth century had tended to be
awkward and heavy. He put out an arm to help stabi-
lize Sarah—what was her name in this time? Caroline
Carelias. She was a vital part of the mission because
she was the contact who would be trusted—

She seemed a bit startled to get any help from him,
and he abruptly realized that she hadn't gotten along
with him at all well in their previous acquaintance.

Oh, gosh, it was just going to stay busy for a while
here. The senior officers and the black Union agent
who was dressed as a slave all came aboard, and the
skipper of the *Jones* cast off the painter of the boat.
Samson and Matt Perney—Jim Strang, his memories
whispered, his name is Jim Strang—pulled at the oars.
The major took the tiller, and they were headed for
shore.

Well, all right, then. If Samson was going to be
functioning as an outboard motor, he was going to
have at least a few minutes to think, and that was what
he needed. First, quick review of personnel here.
There was himself—First Lieutenant Sean Toole, New
York Mounted Rifles, currently detached to the First
D.C., secretly holding the rank of detective in the Se-
cret Service, actually First Lieutenant Prescott Heller,
VMI Volunteer Company, currently assigned to the
Submarine Battery Service, CSN. No wonder he'd

been having so much trouble figuring out who he was!
The rest of the group was Jim Strang, a lieutenant in
the First Missouri Volunteers and Sean Toole's best
friend; Peter Eilemann, a civilian senior detective in
the Secret Service; the major, Roger Eliot, commander of the mission and another of the First Missouri Volunteers; Juky—like most slaves, he had no
more name than that—who had been, at various
times, a slave, an escapee, a conductor in the Underground Railroad and a Union secret agent; and Caroline Carelias.

Hers was a name somebody might recognize, he realized, not for her sake, but because her father was
Telemachus Carelias, editor of the Athens, Alabama,
Weekly Crusader, a newspaper that had been anti-
secession before the war and one of the most prominent advocates of unilaterally surrendering and
rejoining the Union until he was arrested two years
earlier during Jefferson Davis's crackdown.

Well, two men were from the First Missouri. In a
sense that was another one of Samson's old outfits,
"Doniphan's Thousand," the force he had served with
during the Mexican War when his name had been
Hiram Galt.

And now, at last, having time to think, he realized
their mission was—

With a roar like all God's cannon, the USS *Commodore Jones* blew up.

Samson saw it happen because, pulling at the oars,
he was facing that way. Behind him, Jim Strang, pulling on the forward oars, gasped.

The little ship, smaller than a Coast Guard cutter in Samson's own time, had been working her way forward gingerly on the placid surface of the James, gently illuminated by the afternoon sun at one moment, and in the next had vanished in a great red blast.

Where she had been, water fountained up two or three stories high, and above that, high in the sun, Samson could see tumbling boards and wood...

And other things, things he didn't wish to think about, things like a severed human arm silhouetted against the sun for a moment before it tumbled into the water not far from the boat.

The wave came next, a rock-hard shove against the soles of their feet through the wooden planking of the rowboat, followed by the hard buck and plunge of the boat as more waves threatened to capsize her. But Major Eliot knew his stuff, and he got her stern to the worst of it, so that it was merely the worst roller-coaster ride Samson had ever taken.

"Goddamn rebel torpedos," Peter Eilemann swore under his breath. Debris and wreckage was now raining down around them. They all bent forward and covered themselves with their hands as the worst of it hit. From the corner of his eye, Samson saw something big and heavy plunge into the water, making a brief spout. He was already trying to persuade himself that it had been a log, a piece of the gunboat's timbers, a sack of flour from the ship's stores—anything except a human torso still wearing most of its shirt.

"Don't break your cover, men," the major whispered urgently. "In not many minutes the Rebs will be down here to see what they bagged. We won't have the hours we were expecting before we meet up with a patrol. We'll shove the boat off and set it ablaze the instant we're ashore, but if they see us doing that we're all dead men."

They all nodded once, hard.

Bad spot, Samson thought. Good officer. And for once his past life hadn't been a complete public disgrace, so Samson would be trusted and able to be effective from the first.

It looked like trouble, but he'd seen worse.

A few minutes later they were pulling the boat in between overhanging willows, putting themselves out of sight. The baggage was flung helter-skelter onto the bank, with no time to sort or arrange. Samson boosted Caroline over to Jim Strang, standing in knee-deep water, who set her on the bank. Major Eliot, rummaging in the supplies, found a bottle of lamp oil and dumped it into the now-empty boat, then drew out a match from his waterproof container, struck and flung it in. The oil in the bottom of the boat flared immediately, sending red flames up from one end to the other.

Samson, Eilemann and Strang stepped again into the water and shoved the little boat hard, so that it slipped out past the encircling willows and was caught by the current. In a moment it was just one more piece of blazing wreckage on the river's surface.

"Near thing," Major Eliot muttered. "And we may not be out of it yet. All right, divide your loads and shoulder up, boys, we've got Richmond to make by tomorrow morning."

A few minutes later they were on the road. The James was off to their right, due east. They had come ashore just beyond Trent's Reach, a broad part of the river just before Osborn's Bend. So, assuming that Baker had managed to provide them with accurate maps, this must be the Old Stage Road, from which they could cross over to join the Richmond Turnpike in a couple of miles. After that it would be only about ten miles to the outskirts of Richmond.

Call it twelve miles in all. Heck, in three, maybe the water would be out of their boots.

He realized, too, what made that urgent. The farther away they got from the point where they had come ashore, the less likely they were to be connected with anything anyone might have seen.

Now, as for the mission—

He couldn't understand why he was feeling so angry and disgusted. He was sorry about the crew in the gunboat, seventy good men dead—

No, he wasn't.

Here he was with immigrant trash, a traitor bitch and a nigger.

The thought was so startling that it took Samson a moment to recognize its source.

Always before, he had been welcomed by the people he had been in his past lives. Jackson Houston, his World War II identity, had been a thief and a cheat, but had known he could have been better and had welcomed Samson's help in putting things right. Hiram Galt had been a drunken braggart, only too glad to be made into a real hero.

But Prescott Heller was a proud Southerner, devoted to slavery and secession. He didn't want an all-American abolitionist in his head, least of all one who was going to take over his mission and prevent the planned betrayal.

It seemed that while Samson had been probing Heller's memories, Heller had been probing Samson's and gotten to know him thoroughly, with no secrets left unrevealed.

The fact that Daniel Samson had had black friends, even a black roommate for a while, and that the two people in the party who were old friends of Samson's had also had black friends actually disgusted Heller, as well as the awareness that the war would be lost and that the Confederacy was as good as dead—all of this had enraged Prescott Heller to the screaming point.

Tough shit, kid, Samson thought to himself. This time we go through on the right side.

Heller's reaction, deep within his mind, seemed to be shocked beyond all belief. The right side? Who had invaded whom? And who had merely exercised a right of peaceable secession that was obviously there in the Constitution, and then only in defense of the same sacred right of property for which the Founding Fathers—

Tough shit again, kid.

Samson was realizing that where he had been nauseated by Houston and Galt at first, this past life made him burn with hatred. He had seen enough of how slavery really worked and what it was like. And he had fought in three wars and two centuries for the United States, not for a broken-off rump of it. This mission, if Samson had anything to do with it, was going to succeed.

Now just what the hell *were* they supposed to get accomplished?

It took him a moment to wrest the idea out of Heller's memories. Somehow it was actually painful to do so.

Strang looked over at him closely and said in a Southern accent, "Y'all all right, Lieutenant?"

"Yeah," Samson said, using Heller's natural voice. No wonder the guy had become so useful to Lafayette Baker. He could certainly pass for a Southerner easily enough. "Just the heat getting to me. Be fine once the sun goes down."

He could feel Heller's boiling resentment of Strang, and after a moment he identified the source. Strang was a Missourian, from a slave state, though he was no friend of slavery. Older than Heller by a few years, Strang had crossed over into the Kansas Territory and ridden with the Jayhawks, the antislavery irregulars in the border war that had blazed there in the late 1850s as a bloody prelude to the Civil War itself.

Heller thought of him as a traitor.

For the rest of it, in Prescott Heller's assessment, Eliot, another Missourian, was thus another traitor;

Eilemann, a German Catholic by birth, was a disgusting immigrant, the kind that the Northern Factories would flood the pure white American race with if they got a chance...

And Caroline Carelias was...was...

Samson almost had to laugh. Heller was a normal enough teenager in some ways. Heller's raging teenage hormones were killing him. Even with her tendency toward wearing long skirts and sweatshirts with high-top sneakers, Sarah had been the most beautiful woman on earth in Samson's completely prejudiced opinion.

And he had only met Sarah after they were both well over thirty. Every so often, wistfully she had told him she wished they had met much sooner. Although she certainly knew she was still beautiful, there had been a time when she had been breathtaking. She had been a prom queen, Panhel Queen at college, and had won a couple of beauty contests before deciding—typically for Sarah—that it was "all bullshit anyway." Samson had seen pictures....

Well, here she was, physically sixteen or seventeen, the first flush of womanhood on her, and absolutely, captivatingly, a heartbreaker. She might even be a bit improved on the original, depending on what you liked. Either the corset was doing her a big favor, or somehow or other she wasn't quite physically identical to her previous incarnation, as Samson and Turenne and now Matt Perney had always been. To his sour amusement, he realized he was refraining from thinking it because he knew Sarah would have been annoyed and Prescott Heller shocked. Although in every other respect Caroline Carelias looked exactly like Sarah, the 1860s version had quite a spectacularly large chest. Maybe the diet or something was different.

Poor Heller was by no means immune, and yet here was a Union spy from Alabama. He had tried to make do by fantasizing about—

Samson stumbled, which helped cover the look of disgust. It figured. Heller had been fantasizing about taking young Caroline Carelias out in the woods and beating, raping and strangling her.

Think that way once again, Samson thought hard at his past life's mind, and I will—

You'll what, Yankee nigger-lover? We're in here together.

Unfortunately it was true.

Heller's laughter had a ragged, nasty edge that infuriated Samson.

To distract this ugly inner self, he probed again and found yet another focus of hatred. Juky. The compact, wiry man had earned Prescott Heller's hatred for a thousand offenses: being able to read and write, being dignified, being wise in planning and courageous in action. Nothing inflames the hatred of a bigot half as much as the perception that one of the "inferior" people may just be the better man.

It's a shame he didn't lay your mother and get some decent genes into your family bloodline, Samson thought spitefully at Heller. It was petty, but it was certainly satisfying.

It was also a mistake. Suddenly Samson had what felt like the worst cluster headache in human history as Heller threw a screaming, raging temper tantrum inside his head. It was all he could do to keep from clawing at the top of his skull, trying to tear his own brains out. Now that the sun was going down, the sunken dirt roadway was a pleasant enough place, with long cool shadows and little dapples of golden sunlight reaching across it, the deep blue of a Virginia spring evening sky arching over it and the distant murmur of the James mixed with the singing of the birds.

But though he could perceive all of it, he could enjoy none of it because of the howling rage in his mind, and Heller assaulted him with a hundred ugly pictures of Caroline in agony.

All right, damn it, truce! Samson thought, and slowly the storm and tantrum in his mind quieted.

He had just a few moments to draw peaceful breaths before the Confederate cavalry troop showed up on the road ahead of them, riding over the high bridge across the ravine carved out by Proctor's Creek.

Well, they had known that they would have to get past several patrols, and their papers were all in order.

There was a thunder of hooves behind them, and suddenly he knew the game was up. One Confederate patrol riding down toward where a torpedo had gone off, to see if it had been effective and to pick up any survivors or worthwhile salvage, would be perfectly normal, but another closing in from behind could only mean that Confederate forces had known a party had gone ashore and had gone around the long way to trap it.

Still, Major Eliot did his best to bluff them. The captain of the cavalry was peremptory about demanding to see the orders, but the major behaved as might have been expected of an innocent man, obviously convinced that this was merely an extremely inconvenient and annoying mistake.

If there had been any doubt in the Confederate captain's mind, it all might have worked, but there was none. As Eliot was going through his tenth or twelfth explanation, expostulating wildly the whole time and dropping hints about political contacts in Richmond, quite suddenly the captain struck him full across the face with his riding crop. It made a slick, wet, nasty sound and drew blood from one cheek, up across the major's nose, and all the way up his forehead.

It was obviously a signal. With a slam of a rifle butt, a sergeant felled Eilemann from behind an instant later.

But something in the bare beginnings of that motion had triggered Samson into action, so that by the time the impact was driving Eilemann's head forward, he was already half-turned around and saw it only from the corner of his eye. Without looking to see what was coming, Samson pivoted and roundhouse-kicked the horse of the Confederate trooper standing next to him, causing it to shy and rear. The blow aimed at his head went wild, and the Confederate trooper fell from his horse.

Still spinning, Samson brought his other knee into the fallen Confederate's face, throwing his head back in a bloody spray of broken nose and teeth and taking him out of the fight. He continued his pivot, bringing up his Springfield with both his hands to block a descending saber cut, then ducking and firing, bringing down another trooper who was rushing into the fight.

Unfortunately the Springfield was a single-shot muzzle loader, so that was it for firearms. Drawing his bowie knife, Samson lunged in yet another direction, catching a corporal off guard and giving him a brutally hard cut in the belly. But an instant later strong, muscular arms were clutching both his wrists, and in a moment he had been gang tackled to the ground.

It looked as though Strang had awarded one of the enemy a black eye, in addition to what Samson had done, but these were all minor things. The enemy had won completely.

If anything could have convinced Samson that the recent experiences were merely a nightmare of his damaged brain, the next few minutes might have. The Confederate captain read a brief order from General Mosby aloud, the general trend of which was that the captain was allowed to hang obvious spies and federal agents without the bother of a trial. As he did this, his men fastened manacles on all of Samson's comrades, including Caroline, and began to bind their feet together with ropes.

They seemed to be leaving Samson alone, with six men holding him down, until there was enough help to finish the job of tying him up, but the captain obviously regarded this as an admission of weakness. As soon as the other prisoners were bound, he detailed the six holding Dan to the ground to "strip off their Confederate coats and anything else useful you want, and string 'em from the bridge. Get back to bivouac before curfew. And hang the girl but don't let me hear that any of you were less than a gentleman to her."

Hurray for chivalry, Samson thought. He was tempted to complain that one of the men holding him was stroking his leg, not because it was true but just to see if he could cause some trouble. But it didn't seem like the type of trouble he wanted to cause.

In a thundering cloud of dust, the Confederate cavalry was gone.

"Y'all heard the cap'n," the sergeant who had Samson's right arm said. "Bedders and Johnston, you two get them others hung and get me some manacles."

"There's an extra pocket inside my blouse, left side under my arm, where there's some orders you ought to read," Samson breathed softly.

The sergeant said nothing but he stiffened. He had heard. "You two help 'em out. I reckon the fight's gone out of this Yankee," he said. That left just two men holding Samson's arms. They brought him forcibly to his feet.

For the first time he could see clearly what was happening. The detail of six men wasn't about to take any chances with the bound men. They put a noose around the major's neck, tied the other end to the bridge rail, and dragged him to the bridge by the rope around his neck, choking him and inflicting horrible pain as he was dragged along on his face.

Samson kicked and bucked, but his hands were bound behind his back and his feet were tied. It only took them a moment to heave the major over the rail. There was a sick moment while the rope slid easily over the railing, and then it snubbed tight with the horrible crunch of the major's spine breaking. His body swung back and forth, a grisly pendulum above the ravine.

Without much noticing or caring what they had just done—these were obviously seasoned troopers, and this sector of the war had seen far more than its share of guerrilla operations with all the brutality and cruelty that implied—the Southerners dropped the loop around Eilemann's neck.

With the cover blown, Eilemann had begun to pray in German. It took Samson a moment to realize that it must be the Hail Mary that he was going through, sometimes in German, then again in Latin, over and over hysterically. When they began to drag him by his neck and his voice was cut off, it left a sudden silence in which the scraping along in the dirt, then the awful drumming of his bucking body on the bridge and finally his scream of "Jesu!" as he got air back for the single second during which they lifted him up and heaved him over echoed through the shadows of the dying day.

There was another grim crunch, and the expedition was down from six to four members.

At last the sergeant had reached for the pocket Samson had described to withdraw the orders.

"Sarge," one of the privates said, clutching the struggling Caroline by the arm, "I reckon this one's a virgin. Seems a shame to send her over that way. And after we string her, who's going to tell?"

The sergeant barked in fury, "You heard the captain, you damned mountain-blood animal, and—"

He had jerked around to bellow the order, and that gentlemanly response earned him a quick and merciful death. For one instant the sergeant's grip relaxed at the same time as the private holding Samson's other arm adjusted his hold.

With all the concentration brought on by years of *ninjutsu* training, Samson stepped back, letting his muscles go perfectly slack for a bare split second, withdrawing his arms "through the thumbs." Then he wheeled, driving a savage elbow into the sergeant's left kidney, hard enough to burst it and turn it into one huge internal hemorrhage, spinning the sergeant around into a perfect shock-punch to the sternum delivered by Samson's right hand. It was hard enough to crack the ribs, stop the man's heart and force much of his blood out through his ruptured kidney. He was probably dead before he ever knew what had happened, certainly before he hit the ground.

The private had only time to reach down for his rifle before the toe of Samson's boot crushed his temple with savage force.

Two down, four to go, no allies. Samson plunged forward into the dusty road in the *chugari* roll, presenting a poor target for the Minie ball that plowed the dust a few feet behind him.

He grabbed the rifled musket from the ground as he rolled and finished with a flop onto his stomach. He brought the weapon to bear, saw the Confederate trooper drop the rope tied around Juky's neck and bring a revolver up. He killed the Southerner with a shot that went into his forehead just above the right eyebrow and blew the top and back of his head into an instant gory mess behind him.

Three. No more weapons to hand.

He was rushing forward when the shot went off behind him, and one guard fell over abruptly in front of him. There was another bang from behind, and he hoped that, too, was from his side, because as he leaped for the remaining Southerner the man was bringing up a single-shot pistol.

It went off with a roar as if Samson had had his head inside a cannon, but it missed. In the Mexican War, Samson had carried just such a pistol, and the troopers swore that the only way to get a kill with it was to shove it into the opponent's belly before pulling the trigger. He was glad the weapon was still living up to its reputation.

He had just an instant for the thought before he was on his opponent, and at that moment the man drove forward with a bowie knife.

Samson's left hand snapped down, covering the wrist, as he stepped wide to his opponent's right. Then he bent the arm back against the elbow joint, jerking with all his force so the man would have no chance to relax or withdraw and thus absorb any of it. The arm broke with a crunch of cartilage, and the knife fell from the limp hand as Samson continued the motion, forcing the back of the man's head into the hard-packed ground with the full force of Samson's shoulder applied against the man's nose.

Probably he fractured the enemy's skull, but he had already snatched up the bowie knife as he let go, and he plunged it deep into the man's chest before looking up to see what else was going on.

There were no living Confederates left.

He had seen one of them fall. There was an opening in his throat like a ragged, o-shaped mouth, and blood was puddling under his body. At a greater distance, in front of Caroline, was another body sprawled backward. This one was clearly shot through the chest, mouth still open in surprise.

He had just assumed that somehow Jim Strang had also gotten free and gotten hold of a gun as the explanation for the shots, but to his deep surprise—and Prescott Heller's complete shock—Strang, shaking with frustration, was still kicking on the ground, trying to get out of the restraints.

Juky, of course, was still thrashing, the noose around his neck, though he had managed to wriggle enough to be able to breathe.

And Caroline was standing there, one long-barreled pistol lying at her feet, another still smoking in her hand.

"How did you—?"

"Southern chivalry," she said with a sigh. She had an amazingly fetching upper-class Southern accent. "Some of them still believe in it, anyway. They hadn't tied my feet, and my hands weren't tied tightly. And they hadn't searched where I had my dueling pistols hidden." She blushed violently. "Though it's a common enough place for their own smugglers."

It took Samson a moment, but then he joined Strang and Juky in the uproarious laughter, with a little bit of an extra joke in it from Samson's standpoint.

No wonder she'd seemed well endowed. During his time in the federal Secret Service, he'd lost count of how many smugglers they'd encountered wearing "tin-fronted" corsets. The women's clothing of the day provided room to hide a virtual arsenal, or several hundred pages of drawings and photographs, or enough quinine for three companies of Confederate troops, or thousands of dollars' worth—at the black-market price—of gold or silver. Things could be attached to the rigid hoops of the petticoat to hang down inside, or used as stuffing for the immense bustle, which was sometimes as big as a sofa cushion. Or, if quick access was needed, as it obviously had been for these dueling pistols, weapons could be stuffed into the metal breast cups of the rigid corset.

A stray thought crossed Samson's mind: this young woman probably really was physically identical to Sarah. Just as suddenly he had the thought that there might be some hope of getting to find out.

Prescott Heller was obviously disgusted, but since his total body of sexual experience had been the attempted rape of one of his father's slaves—for which he had received a good thrashing—Samson didn't weigh his opinion into the matter much.

He stooped to cut Juky free. He sat up, rubbing his neck and groaning as Samson went on to free Strang.

There was really no point in checking Eliot or Eilemann, but he did briefly. Their necks had broken in the long drop, and they were quite dead. It had been quick, and perhaps the major had been unconscious from the strangling he'd gotten, having been dragged on the ground.

"Cut 'em down," Strang said. There were tears running down his face. "Cut 'em down and let 'em drop. I know we ain't got time to bury 'em, but don't leave 'em up here for the Rebs to brag about. The major, he wouldn't want his body giving them no help." Strang broke down, weeping like a child. Samson threw an arm around him instinctively and led him aside, getting him to sit on the ground. The Heller part of his mind remembered that Major Eliot had been virtually a second father to Jim Strang.

Caroline squatted beside him in a distinctly unladylike way, holding Jim's hand and whispering to him.

It occurred to Samson that at least this trip out he had someone along whom he had always been able to count on to do the right thing, in the life where he had originally known him, anyway.

"Juky," he said, "are you in any shape to give me a hand?"

"Yeah, boss. Gonna have a real bad sore throat, though."

The job was an ugly little nightmare, not made any nicer by the fact that he knew Strang and Caroline could hear the whole thing. At first they thought it would be two quick strokes—Samson had been able to pry the knot loose enough to slide off Juky's head, and it had not been pulled all the way tight yet, but cutting through it with the full weight of a corpse on the other end was something else entirely, especially since the knots themselves were overhead. They ended up sawing through it slowly.

"Hard way to go, Massa," Juky remarked. "Hard way to go."

"You don't have to call me Massa," Samson said.

"We are undercover," Juky said, speaking very carefully and precisely, but keeping his voice barely more than a whisper. "I don't talk like that normally, Sean, any more than you have a Southern accent. But I do have to stay in practice. Staying in practice kept me alive through five years on the Railroad.

"But God love you for saying that, all the same. And God love these poor men, too."

Samson's memory flared for a moment, and he realized that Prescott Heller was outraged. It took him a moment to realize that this was because in private Major Eliot had expressed the opinion that what really mattered was saving the Union, and only that. "Hell—" he could hear the Missourian's drawl in memory "—I guess if we got to free the niggers to do it, the old Union's worth it, but I'll be damned if I can like that idea."

He wondered if Juky knew how Major Eliot had felt, and whether that would have mattered to Juky.

At last they hit on the trick of having Samson, with his two hundred thirty-five pounds of muscle, haul the line tight and hold it still while Juky sawed through with the bowie knife. Instead of impossible, it was merely difficult. First Eilemann, then Eliot, fell in a crash of underbrush into Proctor's Creek ravine. Chances were they'd be found soon. If nothing else, Ben Butler and the Army of the James were slated to come up this way, so probably either a Union company seizing the bridge or a Confederate one hacking it down would find the bodies and give them a decent burial within the week. And chances were it would not take that long. Though the Old Stage Road was little traveled in wartime, most likely someone would come along before then and find the six dead Confederates, and in the process of getting them investigated and buried, Eliot and Eilemann would also get a decent burial.

"Let the dead bury the dead, like Jesus said," Juky whispered. "It's bothering you, ain't it?"

"Yep. It'll bother Jim more, though. Let's get another couple miles, even if we have to do it in the dark. We've got to get some distance between us and this, even if it's only so we can claim we have no idea who killed these Rebs."

Rebs. Prescott Heller didn't like that word, so Samson thought it at him a couple more times.

It was full dark by the time they lay down, off the road in a small cluster of trees. Gallantry being what it was, Samson and Jim Strang had insisted on pitching a tent for Caroline, but the instant they were done, they and Juky stretched out on blankets on the ground, sound asleep immediately. Samson's last thought was that in a minute, just as soon as he felt one bit better, he would get up and take the first shift as guard.

2

Samson woke with a start and a gasp.

Nothing was wrong, except that the training and experience of three wars in two centuries was screaming that he had slept all night behind enemy lines and no one had been on guard. He sat up, chuckling ruefully to himself and looked around. They had picked a reasonable enough campsite, all things considered. Unlikely for snakes, reasonably dry, off the road and out of sight.

He stood up, pulled his Confederate blouse from the bush it had been hanging from and took stock. Plenty of water was still in the canteen, so he had a long drink of it, slipped behind a bush, and relieved himself.

He'd dreamed strange dreams throughout the night, dreams that seemed to come from ten thousand years ago, dreams that said that all these were merely the shadows of the real fight....

He'd flashed through many lifetimes he had yet to visit, marched with Caesar in Gaul and died beside Crassus in Parthia, held on at Thermopylae and around Braddock's blazing wagons, fought the last desperate action to rescue the Maid of Orleans and stood his ground with the pikemen in the bloody mud of Agincourt. He had died more times than he could easily count in those dreams, and he knew on some level, somewhere, that all these dyings were yet ahead of him.

He shuddered. He would have trouble enough not dying, at least until his mission in this time was done.

In May in Virginia, he might have expected a little chill still in the morning or at least heavy cold dew. But this was an unseasonably warm spring—part of the reason hopes for success were so high with Butler's "back door" attack up the James—and the air was already thick and hot. At least no one would feel too much need for a fire, because it would probably be best to get farther away from the fresh corpses up the road before meeting anyone.

He splashed a little water from the canteen onto his face, pulled out a signal mirror to check his hair and decided that pulling a comb through it right now would be more pain than it was worth, so he snugged his cap on.

Now, just what was his mission?

That was really two questions, as he had learned in his last life. There was what he was supposed to be doing *in* his past life, namely the orders from his superiors, and there was what he was supposed to be doing *about* his past life, which called for finding out the flaw at the core of that life and cleaning it out.

This time, he realized, it was three questions. There was what he was supposed to be doing for the Confederacy, what he was supposed to be doing for the

Union, and again that nagging problem of finding out and fixing whatever had gone wrong with his past life.

For once the last seemed the easiest. Whenever he reached down into Prescott Heller's mind and memories, it felt like sticking his hand into a jar of live snakes.

The fact that he disgusted Heller just as much was a source of some satisfaction.

It seemed to him that there was something important about all that, something he should pay attention to, but he couldn't think what it was.

Anyway, now that he had time to think, at least he knew what the missions were. He could remember now—

My God, my God, I stood face-to-face with Abraham Lincoln. The thought moved him almost to tears.

When he and Jim Strang had answered the summons to Lafayette Baker's office, they had been a bit nervous, but since the whole U.S. Secret Service in the Washington area was only about a thousand men, all of them had met Baker a few times.

Which was why they had been nervous.

Baker was physically a big, strong man in his own right, with a bushy beard and mad staring eyes that seemed to bore right through you. Over his desk, he had hung a plain wooden sign: Death To Traitors. That position seemed moderate compared to the way Baker pursued his duties: he often personally led raids and arrests, and more than once had shot it out with Confederate agents within blocks of the White House. His cousin, Stan, a quiet, gentle, modest man who was also one of the Secret Service's most trusted agents, had been heard to comment that Lafayette Baker was a man who was willing to listen to anything from an agent as long as it was "Yes, sir, right away."

But when they arrived at the office to find Major Eliot and Senior Detective Eilemann already there, they had another surprise.

Everyone knew, of course, that the President was fond of just dropping in on subordinates and that he and Baker were personally close, but still it was something to find himself in that room and to have that big, kind, ugly face grinning into his own. Tall men were rare in this time, and Samson was the only man in the room who could look Lincoln in the eye.

"If you'd consider losing seventy pounds, gaining forty years, and getting a damned sight uglier, Lieutenant, I might be able to pass you off as me. You're from the New York Mounted, I believe?"

"Detached from it, sir."

"Fine regiment. I've read the dispatches, and there's nobody I'm prouder of." And quite casually Lincoln rattled off the record of the Mounted Rifles, referring to a couple of specific incidents that had been big in the papers.

Prescott Heller had smiled at that, and had been a little chagrined to discover that he enjoyed getting praise from "that baboon in the White House," as he had endeavored to think of him—without success, for it was really hard not to like Lincoln.

Good, Samson commented, as he read through the memory. At least you responded like a human being.

The revulsion that Heller felt, looking into Samson's mind and seeing what the twentieth century had come to think of Lincoln, was deeply satisfying. But Samson returned to the memory....

The President's attention had next focused on Jim Strang. "Wheat country up where you live, son?"

"Yes, sir," Strang said.

"North Missouri, I'm told. Get yourself through this war alive, and then head west. We need farmers out there in Kansas and Nebraska and Dakota Territory. Soon as we get this war over with, there's a country to build."

"Yes, sir," Strang repeated. He seemed pretty pleased and happy to be there to say it.

Lincoln looked around the room at the four assembled members of the First D.C. and their chief. "Looks like a sound enough crew, Baker. Why don't you fill them in, and I'll just add a word now and again to it."

Baker nodded. "It's really very simple, gentlemen. Your orders are to get into Castle Thunder, make contact with about half a dozen political prisoners who are being held under close guard, break those prisoners out and get them on the road, either back to their homes directly or across the lines back to Washington. You have whatever resources you need to draw on."

There was a long pause, during which everyone looked to Major Eliot to figure out what their reaction ought to be.

The silence was first broken by Lincoln. "Cousin Lafayette, you'll pardon my mentioning that it wouldn't be a bad idea if these men knew why they were going out with a one-in-ten chance of coming back alive." Baker started to speak, but Lincoln waved him to silence and said, "It's this way, gentlemen. The South looks tough as ever right now, but the fact is she's bleeding to death, or so Messrs Baker and Pinkerton inform me. She's going to come apart all at once sooner or later, especially now that I've got myself a general that fights."

Grant the drunk, Heller had thought, helpfully.

"Well, when she goes to pieces, it will help a great deal if the federal armies can come into large parts of her not as conquerors but as a matter of right. I've maintained right along that no state had the right to leave the Union, so therefore none of them *has* left the Union. Officially what we have here is a little problem with collecting taxes and delivering mail in one part of the nation. It would be best of all if our troops were actually invited into some areas to support loyalist governments.

"Now, the reason Castle Thunder is guarded as tight as it is, is because old Jeff Davis has locked up every loyal Unionist he can manage there. Most of these men are leaders in their home communities. What they're in the pen for is being loyal Americans. If they happened to get home just when the fortunes of the Confederacy were suffering some setbacks— when, let us say, they had lost Richmond or Atlanta, for example—it might just be possible that there would be a domestic uprising in one or more of the Southern states. I can only ask you to imagine what the effect would be if, say, Georgia, Alabama or North Carolina were to suddenly switch sides. What the Army of the Cumberland is trying to achieve at a fearful cost in blood might be won overnight. Indeed, it might be enough all by itself to tip over one or more additional states to the Union side and end the war right then. And to have the secession collapse internally would be far better than to have it beaten down from outside.''

Heller's heart had been hammering madly after that, and small wonder. From his viewpoint the proposal was to free the most prominent traitors to the South so that they could stab it in the back.

Samson, as he reviewed this memory of Heller's, reminded himself that it was the spring of 1864. Half a dozen of the bloodiest battles of the war hadn't been fought yet. Sherman hadn't marched through Georgia. Sheridan hadn't burned down the Shenandoah Valley. Troops hadn't gone through nine months of trench warfare at Petersburg . . .

Lincoln hadn't been assassinated.

Peace now, while there was still so much to be saved.

But he hadn't yet been part of Heller's mind at the time, and all Heller did within the private recesses of his mind was to sneer and to think how old and tired Lincoln looked now, how another year of war would surely kill him.

Juky and Caroline had been added to the mission later. Juky was with them because with his knowledge of the Railroad's still-existing safe houses and routes he would be essential in getting the escapees back to their home areas, where local citizens could be counted on to defend them and keep them from being rearrested. Caroline had been her father's messenger in the illegal Peace Society, the biggest resistance group in Alabama, Mississippi and Georgia, a powerful organization with many thousands of members, some of them even Confederate officials and army officers if the rumors were to be believed. Caroline knew the whole elaborate system of signs and passwords. If Juky could get the freed captives close enough to home, Caroline could put them in touch with friends and supporters.

The name "Castle Thunder" suggested that it was part of the system of "castles" around Richmond—fortresses built to stop a possible British invasion during the War of 1812, and really such a fortress had once stood there to guard the waterfront from British landings. But in actuality it was a converted tobacco factory. It was almost as difficult a place as if it had been a fortress, for what made a tobacco factory a logical prison was that it normally had very few openings on the ground floor and big open spaces on the second and third floors, so that it was easy to guard the few exits and to watch all of the prisoners. Moreover, Richmond had grown a lot in fifty years, and Castle Thunder was right in the heart of the Confederate capital rather than on the outskirts.

Jim was beginning to stir, and Samson strolled casually toward him. The birds were singing—heck, making an outright racket—and Samson counted five bluebirds, more than he'd ever seen in his own lifetime, just flitting around the clearing. It was hot, and he wouldn't like it much once they were on the road again. But for right now the deep clear blue of the sky and the thick, deep green of the trees and undergrowth was wonderful, too, like a Wyeth illustration in the books Samson's grandfather had had. He could almost imagine Natty Bumppo stepping out of the trees. There was a crisp aliveness to existence that he hadn't felt in ages.

Part of that was his physical age. He'd died as Hiram Galt in the Mexican War in 1847, and simultaneously been born as Prescott Heller, which meant he was seventeen now. Man, it felt weird to be in a teenage body again. He seemed to have shaken off most of the hardships of the day before much more quickly than he'd have believed possible, but on the other hand Samson's emotions seemed to be rocketing around in a way that made him suspect raging hormones. It was even worse, being seventeen at this point in history, because physically that was about the equivalent of fourteen in Samson's own time.

He almost laughed aloud. He had felt the velvet whisper of Prescott Heller rustling around, wandering through Samson's memories, and he suddenly realized which ones were being hauled up for examination. If anyone had told him that one day his memories of high school would be considered pornographic... well, it sure hadn't seemed that way at the time. Discouragingly far from it, in fact. And at least it was something harmless for Heller to preoccupy himself with.

Samson had taken another couple of steps when he suddenly remembered the most important thing about yesterday.

Samson hadn't known about his concealed Confederate orders and pass, which had lured the Confederates close enough for Samson to strike and free them.

When he had told the Confederate officer where the secret pocket was— No, he had *not* told the Confederate officer where it was.

Prescott Heller had.

Always before on these missions, Samson had been able to count on the mind of his past life to have the same objectives he did. It had just been a matter of straightening out what had been bent or damaged. Jackson Houston and Hiram Galt had felt themselves to be defective and had longed to be corrected, and as soon as Samson was with them, they had wholeheartedly joined in getting the job done.

But Prescott Heller didn't think there was anything wrong with being a brutal racist. Heller had been gloating ever since he learned Lincoln was to be assassinated.

And for one instant there, when Samson had been frantically concentrating on finding a way out, Heller had had his chance to try to betray the mission and had come closer than Samson had known was possible.

Worriedly he checked to see if Heller was paying attention to Samson's present thoughts. No, the Confederate double agent was digging around at Samson's long-forgotten memories of having gotten his hand up under Barb Slatkin's miniskirt on the couch in her parents' house one rainy Saturday afternoon. In fact, Samson could feel a little bit of the physical stirring from the memory. There were going to be some definite things to get used to about the teenage body, all right.

He'd been standing here in the middle of the grove, not seeing anything, for a full minute. When he opened his eyes, he saw that Strang was now getting up from the ground and heading over to make use of the bushes. Juky, too, was up and moving, and since virtually nothing other than the tent had been unpacked the night before, they would be able to move along yalmost as soon as Caroline woke.

"Would you gentlemen all mind turning your backs for a few minutes while a lady gets in and out of the bushes?" she asked, poking her head out of the tent.

By then Strang had come back, so he and Samson stood next to each other. Strang gave him a big wink, and since Samson couldn't think of anything else to do, he winked back. He had to admit he was just slightly curious about what she was wearing scampering around in the woods. Prescott Heller seemed to be visualizing something rather like a dressing gown worn over a set of drop-flap long underwear, and appeared to be getting off on it.

Truly there was no accounting for tastes.

In a few moments she announced, "I'm back in the tent, gentlemen." She might have made a pretty good woods scout, because there'd been no significant noises.

Dividing, rolling and packing the tent took Samson and Strang no more than two minutes. Since they hadn't wanted to chance a fire, breakfast was hardtack. Because they were fresh from Washington, the stuff was freshly issued and probably had only been sitting in some contractor's warehouse for a couple of months—so it was hard as a rock but not maggoty.

With that much taken care of, there was the question of how to carry on the mission. "We have to figure that with what they're going to find there at the bridge they'll know pretty quickly that one of their patrols caught spies in rebel uniforms," Strang said. "And that someone killed off the patrol. So they're bound to be looking real close at any unattached Confederate soldier."

Samson nodded. "Trouble is, the way they're rounding up deserters, we don't want to just throw the identifiers away and try to walk in like these are just old clothes. Okay, where do we find clothing?"

"On clotheslines," Caroline suggested. "I know both of you are pretty big and tall, but if we can find anything close enough, I have my sewing kit and we can make it fit somehow."

"Not many clotheslines out here," Strang said doubtfully. "Least there weren't many houses on the ordnance map."

There didn't seem to be any other way, however, so finally they hit on the strategy of having Samson and Strang move along parallel to the road, while Caroline walked in the road with Juky as escort. It looked only slightly unusual for a young girl to be traveling with just a slave as escort, and Juky was able to make it more convincing by playing the role of the loyal old family retainer. "It's funny that they still believe in loyal old family slaves after all the ones who fled North first chance they got," Dan commented.

Juky grinned at him. "They got to believe in it. Otherwise they'd have to believe things they wouldn't like to about themselves."

It worked better than Samson might have thought, because a proper Southern girl's walking dress was such that it was easier for two men of Samson and Strang's size to move through the undergrowth without being noticed than it was for her to walk right up the middle of the road. With a certain sour amusement as he worked his way silently along a deer trail that paralleled the road about ten yards into the brush, he noted that one thing that might well cover any noise he made was the rustling of the crinoline.

When he'd seen pictures from the period, he'd always thought of hoop skirts as gliding quietly along, as if the woman were rolling on casters, and thus he'd always imagined the whole effect was totally sexless. In practice, he realized, hoop skirts rustled and swayed all over the place and constantly threatened to flip up in the slightest breeze. It was pretty hard not to think of the woman underneath.

There were an amazing number of biting flies out this morning, and the uniform was no protection from them whatsoever. In fact, it seemed mostly to give them places to crawl into and hide before getting another mouthful of Samson. Certainly the uniform itself was wretchedly hot, and the boots were a miserably bad fit. He wished devoutly for his old Vietnam fatigues, or even for the buckskins he'd worn under Doniphan in Mexico.

What he really wished for right then and there was the Italian mountain winter. He'd been cold, but nothing had been chowing down on him.

As he moved along, working his way from tree to tree now, he had just enough concentration to spare for his ongoing quarrel with Prescott Heller. Heller seemed to despise everything and everyone that he didn't worship. The Southern leadership were all gods to him, as was his own father, but he could see no good in the courage and loyalty of Jim Strang, couldn't think of Caroline as anything more than a sex object and a "traitor to the cause" and seemed to be disgusted and furious at the existence of Juky. An educated black man with courage and dignity just couldn't exist in Heller's scheme of things.

There was a noise from the road up ahead—horsemen, three or four of them, approaching. Samson crouched low where he could watch Caroline and Juky. Beside him, shoulder touching his, Jim Strang went down to one knee.

"Reb troopers, look like regulars," Strang breathed. "Got a look at 'em through a hole in the bush. Probably they're running all the roads between Lee on the north and Pickett on the south to make sure Butler didn't land anywhere they don't know about."

Samson nodded. A minute later the three men, all in often-mended gray uniforms, rode up to Caroline and dismounted, removing their hats as if they were going into her parlor rather than meeting her on the road.

"Howdy, miss," the leader said. He was a tall, thin man with a drooping mustache. "Pardon my asking, but y'all know there's been some trouble on this road?"

"Trouble? What kind of trouble? My goodness, you men look *so* serious." Caroline's voice betrayed no real worry. Indeed, she sounded more as if she were concentrating on flirting. Samson was surprised to feel a little stab of jealousy. He sternly reminded himself that she was just doing her job, and, the more attention these men paid to her, the less they would to their surroundings.

" 'Fraid it *is* serious," the Confederate officer said. "We'd got word last night that a party'd been seen going ashore from that Yankee gunboat that hit one of our torpedos. And since those gunboats drop off spies the way a dog does fleas, we sent out a patrol with Captain Clemm to find 'em. Captain Clemm said he caught six and left some men with a sergeant to hang them. This morning we found the sergeant and all the men dead, along with two men we reckon they'd hanged for spies before they got surprised themselves. Best guess we can make is there must be a gang of ten, maybe twenty, Yankees out here bush-whacking and raiding. Ain't no kind of road for a woman to be on by herself.''

"Captain *Walter* Clemm?'' Caroline asked. "Not Walter?''

"No, miss, his first name was John. Might be a cousin or something to the one you knew.''

Strang and Samson had glanced at each other. It was obvious that she was delaying for some reason.

Samson looked at Juky and saw his hand patting his leg as he shuffled aimlessly, looking down at his feet in the dirt. The pats could be read in Morse: "H-E-L-P...O-N-E...K-N-O-W-S...M-E.''

The sharp intake of breath at his side told Samson that Jim, too, had read the message. Without hesitating, Samson brought his Springfield up to ready. Strang did the same.

One of the Confederates was behind a horse from them, and the other was blocked partly by a tree. They couldn't get a clear shot. They lowered their weapons and slowly wriggled a few feet forward.

It felt good to be back in action with Matt Perney—though his name was different in this life—beside him.

He sighted in again, but still there was that one behind the horse....

Caroline and the Confederate lieutenant had progressed from discussing which Captain Clemm was dead to trying to work out who might be related to whom. Even Prescott Heller seemed to be a bit amused at the way the two of them had gotten into the process of trying to discover whether or not they might be distant cousins or perhaps have attended parties or soirees at each other's homes. It was a process made more complicated by the fact that the lieutenant couldn't quite bring himself to violate protocol and ask her name, and Caroline, aware that the name *Carelias* would probably be enough to jail or hang her, wasn't volunteering it.

They had clear shots at two of the Confederate troopers, but they needed to be sure what the third was up to, and Samson urged him on in his mind. Come on, come on, come out where we can see you....

"At any rate, miss, we can hardly let an unattended woman walk up a road infested with bushwhackers. I'd appreciate it if you'd accept a ride into Richmond with Struthers here. Your boy can walk behind."

"Oh, but I'm perfectly safe with Juky, I'm sure," Caroline said. "Why, his grandfather was in our family. And they've always been guards for us. Show them, Juky."

Juky drew a huge bowie knife. It was an Arkansas Toothpick like the one Samson had carried in the Mexican War. Juky pointed to a tree on the other side of the road and said, "Second knot on the dead branch, Miss Caroline?"

"Fine, Juky. Go ahead."

His arm snapped out in a sidearm lash like a striking cobra. The dead branch exploded into splinters around the knot, and knife and branch together fell into the bushes.

"Can I fetch it back, boss? Don't want to lose it."

The captain chuckled. "All the same, miss, one faithful nigger's no match for a half a company of Yankees."

"Unless we're talking about romancing or manners or anything as becomes a gentleman," the one behind the horse said.

That brought a guffaw from everyone, including Caroline.

"Sure, y'all can fetch it in, boy," the captain said indulgently, but as Juky turned to retrieve his knife, the one behind the horse said, "Just a minute there."

Quicker than thought, he stepped forward and seized Juky by the ear, twisting it hard enough to bend him over.

"So this here nigger's been in your family all those years, has he?"

"See here, sir, that boy is my property and I won't have you mistreating him!" Caroline's temper flared very impressively, and the captain turned immediately to his man, obviously about to order him to stop, but the trooper was already explaining.

"I hunted bounty a long time, Captain, and this here nigger used to be a number-one man on the Railroad. He done me out of ten bounties at least, and there was a hanging price on him that woulda bought me a good house. Reckon now I'll just have to hang him for the pure pleasure of it and hope I can collect after the war. And as for whatever that wench has been putting on—"

"See here, sir—" Caroline sputtered.

"Forrest, you'd better be sure of—"

"Took me a powerful long time to get a look at this coon's face to be sure, Captain, but he had to look up to throw that knife." Forrest locked Juky's head under his arm and struck Juky full in the face with his free hand, a heavy, thudding noise that Samson felt in the pit of his stomach.

Samson's finger squeezed the trigger, and the captain fell dead, the Minié ball having gone in through the side of his neck and out in a gory spray through his forehead. Beside Samson, a tenth of a heartbeat later, Jim Strang's Springfield barked sharply, and the other man collapsed, a dark spot low on his back and an explosion of red on his chest.

As one, Samson and Strang rushed forward. At the shots, Forrest must have been distracted a second from the beating he was giving Juky. Suddenly Juky broke free and lashed out, driving the Confederate trooper back with a hard left uppercut and following up with a right cross that had Forrest tumbling backward even as Caroline whipped out her dueling pistol and fired.

As suddenly as that, the fight was over. The captain and the other man had been killed quickly and cleanly, almost before they knew there was trouble, but Caroline's aim had been spoiled by Forrest's backward tumbling, and the shot went into his abdomen, making a bloody mess of him without killing him. He lay on his back, choking and pouring blood onto the road, thrashing weakly.

Juky pulled a spare knife from its hiding place in his trouser leg, walked cautiously around to Forrest's head and knelt beside him, gripping him by the hair.

As the knife descended onto his throat, Forrest focused for a moment, snarled "Nigger!" and spit into Juky's face.

An instant later his throat was open all the way to his spine from one ear to the other, and he lay staring at the sky with unseeing eyes.

As Juky stood up, wiping his face, he muttered, "I deserved that."

"Like hell, after what he'd done to you," Strang said.

"No, not for the way I treated him. But way back when I started on the Railroad, I learned you don't get yourself up close to a man like that till you're sure he's dead. I'm just goddamn lucky he didn't have anything worse than words and spit to use on me. Gotta get my main knife from that tree." In a flash he was gone into the brush.

"He's right, you know," Samson commented.

"Yeah, but it still goes hard to hear him say it," Strang said softly. "Guess I can't help how I was raised. But I ain't gonna let him know it bothered me. He's a brave man and a damned fine fighter, nigger or not."

As they were talking, they were reloading. The habits of war didn't let them leave their weapons unloaded for one second longer than absolutely necessary. Automatically Samson pulled a paper cartridge from his case, ripped open the end away from the bullet with his teeth and dumped the powder down the barrel. He brushed the paper into wadding around the base of the Minie ball—which was a misnomer, since it was actually a hollow bullet designed to expand in the barrel rather than an old-fashioned ball—pressed the bullet in pointed end up, swung the ramrod up and in, tamped the bullet down on top of the powder and pulled the ramrod back out, sliding it back into its hinged mount under the barrel. Bringing the Springfield up, he half cocked the hammer, pulled a percussion cap from his cap box and placed it on the nipple. He was ready to fire again. When the occasion came up, he would only have to bring the hammer to full cock and pull the trigger.

It amazed Samson that in Prescott Heller's memory he could find many times that Heller had done the whole complicated operation in battle. The rifled musket was by any reasonable standard an obsolete weapon. Hell, the Jenks carbine he had carried in the Mexican War had been a breechloader that took only a third as much time to load and fire and didn't force you into any dangerous exposed positions while you were doing it. But plenty of the heavy old Springfields were still in service on both sides, and it was still the Confederacy's main infantry weapon. This was once again the result of the basic policy of a democracy at war: anything bright, shiny and new that the generals wanted, anything expensive the contractors wanted to build, but nothing that cost a dime more than it had to for the men who did the fighting. Some things just didn't change.

Oddly enough he had at last found something Heller agreed with him about. Either of them would have given a lot right then to have one of the Secret Service's brand-new 16-shot repeating Henry rifles, and even though the First D.C. had been among the very first units to be equipped with them, on this mission behind enemy lines, it had been more important not to attract any attention. Although it might have been explained as having been taken off a dead Yankee— after all, that was where half the Confederate weapons had come from anyway—it was thought better not to have anything that needed explaining whatsoever.

Now that the Old Stage Road was getting littered with Confederate bodies, however, the idea of being inconspicuous was pretty ludicrous, and Samson really wished he had those extra shots.

Oh, well, nothing to do for it now. Juky was returning with his knife from the underbrush, and the next question was how to conceal the evidence of what had happened, then get themselves as far away from it as possible.

Samson looked at Juky and almost gasped. Forrest's beating had been rougher and harder than he'd realized. Juky's eye was half-swollen shut, his lip was split and the heavy bruise suggested that he might even have cracked a cheekbone. "Better let me have a look at that," he said.

"Happy to, soon as we get someplace away from all this," Juky said. "I know I'm not too good, but I'll be a lot worse if they catch us here."

Strang nodded. "Well, then—"

There were more hoofbeats from the same direction as the others had come from. From the sound of it, it might be twenty horses or more.

"Into the woods, quick," Caroline hissed. "Juky, you stay out here and keep your knife to hand."

There was no time to argue plans. If Caroline knew what she was doing, she was way ahead of Samson. Samson and Strang dived into the underbrush and made themselves invisible right away. Samson hoped Caroline would know what she was doing. So far, the evidence was that she usually did.

The next thing she did was so weird that for a moment he wondered if she'd lost her mind entirely. She flipped her hooped petticoat up so that it all but covered her head, letting her dress fall into a ball inside it, and then scooped a handful of blood from the ground next to Forrest's body. Then she lay down on her back on the ground and smeared the gory mess between her legs and down onto her thighs. She whispered something to Juky, and he was suddenly flat on the ground, to all appearances barely able to raise himself on his hands.

What came around the bend was a full troop of Confederate cavalry, at least seventy men on horseback. This time there were far too many to fight; the odds were not merely long, but hopeless.

As they burst into view, Caroline began to sob.

The troop pulled up, the captain's eyes widening. "What the—?"

"Yankees," Caroline moaned. "Bushwhackers. I was just...just goin' over to visit my auntie, just a little half mile away, and they come up the road while I was talking to the captain...and they...and they..." She clutched the bloody crotch of her pantaloons and wailed.

"Which way did they go?" the captain shouted, his voice tight and his face pale with rage.

She pointed down the road, the way they had come, moaning, "They beat up poor Juky, too, when he tried to stop them."

The captain looked around, seeing Juky struggling in the dust, and now his face was clenched and furious. "Men, you see what the Yankees are really after. Raped a poor girl and beat hell out of the decent Negro that tried to defend her. Cut down three gallant soldiers in cold blood. You all get up on up the road and if you don't have me every one of those bushwhackers hanging from a bridge or a tree by noon I'll by-God know why not." He turned back to Caroline for a moment. "How many were there?"

"Nine of them," she sobbed. "They...they took Juky's little girl, Patsy. Please, Captain, she's only ten—"

As no doubt she had hoped it would be, it was all too much for the Confederate captain. He lost all control and bellowed to the rest of the troop. "All right, men we're after them! Rogers, you stay here and tend to the lady! Come on, men, they can't have much of a start. At a gallop, *now!*"

They were away in a thunder of hoofs and a cloud of dust, gone around the bend in seconds.

Rogers knelt beside Caroline, ignoring Juky. "Help Juky first," she whispered. "Poor thing, I'm afraid they've killed him."

"Now, now," the doctor said, soothing her, "he'll be fine. Negro men are strong as apes. Let's just see."

"I dreamed that the boys were all coming home," Caroline said.

The doctor paused and sat back. "These are gloomy times," he said.

"Yes, but we are looking for better."

"What are you looking for?"

"A red-and-white cord."

"Why a cord?"

"Because it is safe for us and our families."

He reached forward and squeezed her hand. She squeezed back, her fingers moving oddly. "Ha!" he said. "Are you really hurt?"

"Not me, but Juky is."

Instantly Rogers moved to Juky, kneeling in the dirt of the road to take a look at him. "Uh-oh. Do you need to hurry up the road?"

"I'm afraid so," Caroline said.

"Because this bruise around the eye really needs to be drained, and I ought to put a few stitches into your lip, Juky. But that will take a couple of hours and it's likely to hurt, and I can hardly do it here."

Meanwhile, Caroline had signaled Jim and Samson out of their hiding places, and as they approached, Juky managed to say, "There's a place near here we can go, if we have to. Can I keep going without your doctoring?''

The doctor, a very thin man who couldn't be more than twenty now that Samson looked at him closely, bent and looked over Juky's face very carefully, and at last said, ''Maybe for a day at most. You're going to lose sight in that eye from the swelling, most likely within the next hour, and if you get the infection I'd expect, you'll lose the eye and might be down with fever for a month if you live. Always assuming you don't get the lockjaw from the way your lips and tongue are cut up. And that's if your teeth aren't so ruined that you're knocked down by the pain. No, you can't keep going.''

''Can y'all leave me behind—'' Juky started to ask.

''Nothing doing,'' Samson said, and the other two nodded.

''Then I have to swear you all to keep this secret. We're going to a Railroad safe house. It ain't far.''

He led them only a few hundred yards up the road before they turned onto a winding trail through the river bottom. Even by then, Juky's injuries were beginning to take a toll, and shortly Strang was supporting Juky by one arm as they wound their way down into the wet ground near the James.

''How did you know—?'' Samson began.

Caroline shrugged. ''I didn't. But so many of the Southern doctors are Quakers or Brethren that there was at least a chance.''

''Quaker, in fact,'' Rogers said. ''No longer practicing—I think my conscience would let me carry a gun. But not for either side in this war, not to defend the South's slavery and not to defend the North's coercion. And it's not that surprising that I picked up on your sign. I knew more or less that something was up already, so I wasn't surprised to hear you give the sign."

"How did you know?"

"Next time you want to forge a rape, you can't be quite so delicate and ladylike. More blood right over the genitalia and not so much smeared down the legs."

Caroline blushed violently. That was another thing Samson had seldom seen in Sarah. Upbringing did make some difference, apparently.

From in front of them, Juky said, "It's just around this turn. You might have to let me do a little talking first."

The cabin was little more than a shack, but it looked as though at least until recently it had been kept neat and mended. The woman on the porch, washing clothing in a big, steaming wooden tub, stood up and wiped her face with her apron as they approached. She was black, with very dark skin, stout, and somewhere over fifty years old, but so vigorous that she might be almost any age less than that. As they drew nearer and she recognized Juky and saw how badly hurt he was, she gave out a long, low whistle. It might have been just an expression of astonishment, but Samson's trained eye saw movement in the woods around the cabin, and he guessed that they were now being watched through the sights of one or more guns.

Juky murmured something to Strang and the two of them approached the cabin. Rogers, Samson and Caroline hung back to see what happened.

There was a complicated discussion between Juky and the woman, and finally she nodded emphatically, gesturing for all of them to come inside quickly. They hurried in to discover that the large cabin, which appeared to sit on a solid stone foundation, had a concealed cellar.

"Lucky you want it now," the woman said in an accent that didn't sound like Samson's idea of either Southern or black. He knew there were several dialects along the Southern coast with names like Geechee and Gullah, but he had no idea what this particular one would be called. "Sometime come winter there be water to your knees in there. You stay down here. They have the county out and rousted all day, you bet. They be here again and again, you bet. Go tomorrow next day, when you can."

They all nodded. It might not have been how Samson would have put it, but it was dead clear that she knew what she was talking about. She led them down into a stone-walled cellar, fairly pleasant but with a distinctly damp floor and several benches wide enough to sleep on. "Got candles for you," she added, setting a couple of them on nails in boards, "but you don't use them after dark. Not sure there be not a chink hole round somewhere. You get caught, I nice but not *that* nice. You get caught, I never seen you 'fore and y'all swing on a rope."

Her little speech had a kind of recited quality to it that suggested that perhaps she had given it so many times she didn't hear the words herself anymore.

She looked around, was evidently satisfied with their understanding and started up the stairs.

"Thank you very much, ma'am," Caroline said.

Apparently nothing could have startled her more. The woman turned around and dropped a little, hesitant curtsy, then scuttled up the stairs and pulled the wooden planking over the opening. As the planking closed them into the tiny space, Juky spoke. "Hid a lot of people in here over the years. Never thought I'd have to hide myself. Old Ma, she's all right, really. Best there is, but she's got nothing to do with the war. It's the Railroad that matters for her. And she's managed to keep this part of it running, even up to now."

Rogers lit four candles with matches and said, "Toole and Strang, hold him down for me."

"You don't need to do that," Juky said. "I know I have to hold still, and I will."

"This has nothing to do with physical courage," the doctor responded. "As much as this hurts, anyone thrashes around a lot. And we can't have you doing that while I'm punching holes into you around your eye and sewing up your lip. If you don't move, it's less trouble for your friends here, but if you try, they'll be there."

Juky nodded, acquiescing.

Samson winced at the unboiled, unsterilized surgical tools. At least they looked as though they had been kept clean. To drain the hemorrhaged area around

Juky's eye finally required four separate punctures and made a terrible mess. Samson knew a twentieth-century doctor wouldn't have done that, or done it that way, but he had no idea what he would have done. Even if Rogers wasn't doing the ideal thing, he was doing something he knew how to do and that he knew would do some good.

When Rogers was done, Juky seemed to be heading into shock. They wrapped him to keep him warm, but they also took advantage of his unconsciousness to get his lip sewn, as well. It was late in the evening by the time they were done, and Ma had already warned them that the candles had to be out soon.

"Now all he needs to do is sleep, as long as we keep him warm," Rogers said. "I'll take a turn next to him, and if one of you will..."

Samson nodded. "Sure, of course."

Strang seemed a bit baffled, but then shrugged and said, "Reckon a Negro—" He hit the word hard. It might have been the Missouri in his accent or the Missouri in his upbringing, but it came out sounding like *niggero* "—is person enough to be next to under a blanket. 'Specially if it's this one and it's to save his life."

They drew straws. Rogers would go first, then Strang, then Samson. Since they couldn't move until fairly late the next day, they decided to make the watches long enough to allow everyone a couple of long periods of sleep; sleep might be very scarce in the days following.

With his watch hours away, Samson found himself seated on a bench next to Caroline, talking in whispers. There was no question in his mind that this was a past life of Sarah's. He recognized his ex-wife's crusading spirit on behalf of anyone and anything less fortunate than herself, her quick sense of humor that so often could slash like a razor, her keen intelligence. She was sixteen—everyone matured earlier in this century, he realized—and of prime marriageable age, but she seemed to think that was unlikely in her home territory, because "the Confederates won't be married to a traitor and most of the Union loyalists are poor hill folk."

"You have something against poor men?" Samson asked, startled.

"Me? I don't know. I've never been courted by one. But I know they're likely to have something against me, and I won't be married to a man who secretly despises me for my upbringing and looks down on himself and resents me because he didn't have a similar one. Even if he might be right about it, I'm not going to spend the rest of my life feeling ashamed of who I am or where I came from, let alone live in a house with someone who wants to make me feel that way. But I suppose that must sound like the ravings of a lunatic to you, Lieutenant Toole." She moved a little closer to him in the dark. Her crinoline rustled maddeningly.

There was no way to tell her that in the future he would sleep with her every night for several years and wish it had never stopped, but that seemed to be the only thought on his mind. Instead, he asked, "What would I think was crazy about it?"

"It is commonly supposed," she said with heavy sarcasm, "that what a woman wants is a husband. And that *that* is more important than having one who will treat her kindly, or one who likes her as she is."

"I don't suppose women want a husband just to have one any more than men want a wife just to have one," Samson said.

"Oh, but what's so infuriating is that so many women do. There are plenty of old-maid schoolmarms and spinsters who do charitable work and who are productive, valued leaders of their communities—and who would never be able to render so much service if they were married—who nonetheless would happily become much less useful and subject themselves to the treatment of a drunkard, a brute or an idiot just for the extra respect that they can claim by being married. And what is the result, Lieutenant Toole? How many thousands of women end up the wives of absolute beasts because they cannot endure the thought of being looked on as unwanted, even though plenty of honorable and decent work is available to them?"

Dan wasn't sure he wanted to get into a reform campaign. After all, in a certain sense he was a guest in this century. But he had to admit, "There's a lot of sense in what you say, Caroline. I just hadn't thought about it much."

"You really think so?" She sounded astonished. And then, setting Samson's heart racing, she reached over and took his hand. "You aren't just... Oh, never mind, I can tell you're not."

"Tell I'm not what?"

She moved a little so that he could feel a very slight pressure from her shoulder against his, and her tiny hand lay tightly and gently as a butterfly in his big, callused one. "Oh, you know there are some young men who think... well, that the ability in a woman to make conversation or to talk about ideas is like... like playing the piano or having a knack for the right color of wallpaper. A little accomplishment to be praised, but not to be taken seriously. But I can tell you're listening."

Samson smiled in the dark. He doubted Sarah would ever have said that to him, even though he had listened a lot. At least in this century the expectations were lower. "What you say is interesting," he said.

They talked about other things after that, beginning with families. It was clear that Caroline worshiped her father as a hero, but, what the hell, the guy had defied armed authority and angry mobs to print what he felt was the truth, and that was heroic enough. She'd had a brother who had died some years before—of measles, of all things, which obviously was a much more serious business back here than it had been when Samson was a kid, let alone when he'd been an adult and vaccination had practically wiped it out. Her mother had died six summers before, of what Samson suspected was probably plain old amoebic dysentery.

Samson had to wing it a little. His father had died
when he was six, when he had stepped on a Chinese
Communist mine in the long retreat from Chosin
Reservoir, the luck that had gotten him through
Guadalcanal and Iwo finally running out. Instead, he
merely said his father had died when he had been six,
and from his name and the date, Caroline assumed it
must have been during the Potato Famine. He could
hardly tell her that he'd played football in high school
or gone to Indochina. Nor could he tell her that the
day he was set loose wandering in time, he happened
to be in the right place at the right time because he was
participating in a university psychology experiment
since he needed the money after being fired from a job
as a used-car salesman. He did say he'd enlisted in part
because his civilian employer had asked him to do
things his conscience wouldn't let him do, and when
she asked in what industry or field he had worked,
he'd said transportation, and she'd assumed he'd been
a railroad agent.

She admired him greatly for having behaved hon-
orably enough to get fired. Father, it seemed, had always been a passionate foe of the railroads.

Caroline was still very much a girl of her time. It
was most of the way through Dr Rogers's watch before Samson got an arm around her, and he never did
get a kiss. Indeed, for one instant he was afraid she
would slap him when he tried, but she put a gentle
finger on his nose and whispered, "Congress has made
you a gentleman, Lieutenant, and you do not have the
authority by yourself to decide to be anything else."

Even then her voice was pure music to him.

Finally, though, it was late enough that he needed to sleep before his watch. Reluctantly he squeezed her waist again, whispered "Good night" and stretched out on another bench. Just as he was falling asleep, her lips lightly brushed his forehead, and she whispered, "Good night," as well.

It was a good thing he was exhausted. Otherwise, he was quite sure, he'd never have gotten any sleep. As it was, he dreamed of Sarah and of their marriage all night long. The dreams were so vivid that afterward he couldn't entirely sort them out from things that had really happened. He knew that some parts were real; their wedding had happened pretty much that way. He also knew that some parts were just plain false; since they hadn't met before their thirties, they certainly hadn't gone to a high school senior prom together. But which of the conversations, sitting on the king-size mattress and box spring that had been most of the furniture in his old apartment, getting drunk on red wine by candlelight, had been real, and which only in dreams?

As for Daniel Samson, what exactly was "real" and what was "dream," anyway?

3

Samson woke reasonably refreshed and, though dirty and tired of hardtack, not feeling too bad about the upcoming day. The sun rose a couple of hours into his watch, and he was able to light a candle and take a close look at Juky, who seemed to be much better. At least the terrible swelling around the eye was down a good deal. Trails of bloody fluid dried onto Juky's face showed that Rogers had known his business. His lip looked a little better too. None of the cuts or bruises seemed to be swelling up or turning red, the warning signs of a dangerous infection, and that was especially good.

He sat quietly, taking stock. There weren't a lot of options just now. If Ma could get them any kind of clothing...no, not any. They needed to look important enough not to get grabbed by the "dogcatchers," Confederate troops sent to scour the city for draft-age men. Get caught by them, and you were in for the duration.

In the back of his brain, he could find Prescott Heller in a thorough case of adolescent sulks. Samson had to have a little bit of sympathy. After all, the poor kid had been a star student at VMI, had been trusted with and taken on an incredibly dangerous mission on behalf of "his country," as Heller saw it, and now he was stuck as a passenger on Samson's expedition, which he disapproved of in just about every way possible.

He went to check on Juky again, but there seemed to be no change since the last time. Now why was it that in the stuff he'd read as a kid, people never got more banged up than in a playground fight? After the brutal beating he'd gotten in the face, what Juky really needed was a week to recover, and he'd still be sore at the end of it.

It seemed a miracle to Samson that Rogers was able to avoid infections at all, not knowing anything of germs or sterilization. Probably the human immune system was fairly tough to begin with, and then, too, Rogers was clean if not sterile in his working habits.

Caroline had said that because they were antislavery, the Quakers were often strong supporters of the Peace Society, the Order of American Heroes, or the Peace and Constitutional Society, the big pro-Union resistance groups in the South. But because they were pacifists with a tradition of caring for others, many of them had enlisted as medics in the Confederate Army, some of them getting all their training there. Pretty clearly Rogers either had been a doctor before the war or had a lot of native talent.

The thought of being out on the typical Civil War battlefield with no ability to shoot back, trying to save lives with the crude tools of the day—steel that barely held an edge and iron that sometimes shattered under pressure... Samson looked at where Rogers was sleeping and scratched his head. Not that it was a contest or anything, but he was glad he didn't have to face any systematic comparison with Rogers. He wasn't really sure who would come out the better man.

Strang and Caroline seemed to be sleeping comfortably. It was a strange thing, but now that he was meeting them back in this time, he was rapidly beginning to think of his best friend and ex-wife by their names in this lifetime, and not just because he addressed them by those names. It was as if...well, it was certainly the same soul, but just as two cloned plants will grow differently in different soils...

Jim Strang was a good guy, and Samson was glad to be with him, but he had to admit that Prescott Heller had a point. The kid from backwoods Missouri was rougher and cruder than the witty Matt Perney he remembered, but on the other hand he had an automatic self-confidence that Matt had lacked. Apparently growing up on the frontier did more for your attitude than growing up in the suburbs, Samson thought sourly. Which might explain a number of things about the century he had come from.

Caroline, on the other hand... Now that was an interesting question. Sarah had always seemed to be eaten up by doubt and a kind of unfocused guilt that didn't seem to have anything to do with anything she had done. She had never quite seemed to believe Samson when he had told her she was pretty, and had always dressed as if she needed to hide some kind of defect. She had been a joiner and worker on causes—

heck, in some ways it was the crusader in her that he'd fallen in love with—but she had always seemed to wonder if she was doing the right things or enough of them.

Caroline, on the other hand, had grown up as a much-courted young lady and had the kind of automatic faith in her own attractiveness that came with that. No one had treated her intelligence as "weird," though they had ignored it, and though she had had the normal quota of disappointment, she hadn't been discouraged in the way Sarah had been.

Of course there was the other point, as well: the issues of this period were a lot simpler. How could you feel any way different about slavery?

Prescott Heller reminded him that there were people who felt very differently about slavery. For one instant, Heller seemed to surge up in his brain, as if to take over and rush out of the house, and Samson could sense that Heller was visualizing running to a cavalry post and turning in the whole Railroad operation here.

Samson gritted his teeth, bore down and forced Heller back.

Couldn't this passionately patriotic Southern kid even begin to see Juky's courage, decency or intelligence?

He could not, Samson realized. Prescott Heller could see only the skin color, and beyond that nothing mattered. He could even listen, as he had the night before, to Caroline pointing out that most of the plantations were not as old as her grandparents and that the "traditions" the Southerners said they were fighting for had roots an inch deep, but Heller couldn't make the connection that his father had become an "aristocrat" on the strength of having been a real estate dealer and having saved one choice piece of cotton land for himself. The "ancient family estate" had been bought and built less than five years before Heller himself had been born.

When Samson looked up from these thoughts, Master Xi was standing beside him. *You are seeing his tragedy, then. To exist at all, he must believe things that are not true.*

Dan shrugged. That was obvious in and of itself, but it didn't tell him how to deal with Heller. It didn't seem to him that a life could be redeemed against its will. Even if he dragged Heller, kicking and screaming inside, into doing the decent thing at the critical moment, what would that do for his lifetime?

Master Xi smiled at him. *Exactly. And there is an even more difficult question for you... what is it that you need to learn from Prescott Heller?*

Nothing, Samson thought suddenly, and was surprised at the vehemence of the thought. He hadn't minded learning that a cheap hood like Jackson Houston could have redeeming qualities, even if the major one was that he had not been as bad a person as his environment would have dictated. Hiram Galt's easy practicality had been almost a pleasure to absorb.

But what was it that he could get from this snotty little racist?

Exactly the problem, Master Xi said, and vanished.

Strang stirred, and Rogers showed some signs of waking up. It was hours till they could be moving, so Samson sat back, ate some more hardtack and waited for everyone to wake. He could easily believe what he'd heard more than one old campaigner say about hardtack: that it was the best method of exercising the jaw muscles yet devised. On the other hand, the fact that it took so long to consume meant that a meal was always a good way to kill some time.

An hour and a half later, when everyone was awake and had eaten something, except for Juky, they talked over their situation. As a member of the Peace Society, Dr. Rogers was a legitimate member of the group, and besides, they needed his advice about how well Juky would be able to travel.

What they ought to do wasn't obvious at all. If they canceled the mission, they might not get another chance. As the Army of the James closed in from the south and the Army of the Potomac from the north, Richmond would come under siege and the prospects of getting anyone in or out would be fairly dim. Besides, Telemachus Carelias and the others were needed *now,* not in the six months from now that it would take to mount another mission.

But they were down two members from the team originally sent, and Lafayette Baker was noted for sending out missions a little shorthanded anyway. He thought it increased courage, resourcefulness and alertness—and it probably did, in the agents who sur-

vived. There was also little way of telling how completely or quickly Juky would recover, for though
there had been no sign of concussion the day before,
Rogers pointed out that it would not be unusual for
one to develop later.

And without Juky, instead of escaping on the rela-
tively safe Underground Railroad routes out through
West Virginia or northern Maryland with the released
political prisoners heading south into North Carolina
and through the Railroad, they would most probably
have to get out, with the prisoners, through the federal lines down by Bermuda Hundred or up north
where heavy fighting was going on.

Juky woke up briefly while they were talking, and
though he was in terrible pain, he seemed coherent
enough, so probably there was no concussion. They
gave him as much water as he would take and let him
go back to sleep, then continued the discussion.

A further problem with abandoning the mission was
that right now it was going to be difficult to flee in *any*
direction, with or without the prisoners. As long as it
was going to be so difficult to get out, why not try to
accomplish something before they did?

That was Strang's argument, and Samson thought
it made more sense than any other. Just the same,
there was a nagging feeling in the back of Daniel
Samson's mind that there was some important thing
that he knew but was overlooking. He had no idea
what it might be, but somehow there was something
he ought to realize. . . .

They were interrupted when Ma came down the stairs, carrying a large trunk. First she looked in on Juky, and seemed pleased with his progress. "You good doctor," she told Rogers, who bowed as if he were receiving a medal.

Then she opened the trunk and produced a full collection of civilian clothes, even in the right sizes. "Ain't no problem," she explained. "I do wash for white folks, and they just send me up to get from the hampers. So I all alone up there, I go in the cupboard, things from the back they ain't gonna miss, specially not some that's from boys that's dead 'cause the war."

The clothes were new enough and expensive enough for Samson and Strang to be able to pass as well-off young men who might have paid substitutes to take their place in the draft, or who perhaps might be "bombproofs," holders of public offices that exempted them from the draft.

There was new clothing for Caroline, too, a plainer dress than the one she had been wearing, but not road worn and perfectly serviceable. With quiet efficiency, Ma stripped off Juky's bloody shirt, barely waking him up to do it, and took it upstairs to wash, as well. There was nothing in the trunk that would not have been too obviously new and expensive to be on a slave.

With the problem of disguise solved, and the fact that escape was going to be tough no matter what, it seemed as if the only thing left to do was to go on. Samson just wished he could think of what that one reason for *not* going on might be.

Caroline exchanged a pile of memorized, coded messages to and from various branches of the Peace Society with Rogers. Before outlaw radio, Samson realized, a resistance movement was pretty much confined to a system of passing messages over and over, hoping that they would eventually find their way to the right recipients. Undoubtedly some of these messages had already been passed more than once, and others were outdated or were replies that no longer mattered. All the same, the two of them spent twenty minutes reciting to each other to make sure they got them right, because although a large part of the messages were probably unnecessary, neither Caroline nor Rogers had any way of knowing which ones those might be.

When that was done, Rogers took one more look at Juky, gave them a packet of morphine they were to use sparingly on him and turned back to them. "All right, now, the last thing is, we've got to make sure that the story of what was done to this young lady and what condition she's in is kept consistent. I will say that she has recovered fairly completely, although she is now very prone to tears—Miss Caroline, I assume that you can come up with them when needed, since nothing will do a better job of distracting most of our Southern gentlemen—and because she is quite sore and in danger of hysteria, she may occasionally behave very badly. That should give you a bit of license should you need it. Emphatically, however, you are *not* an invalid, since we don't want to have to explain what you are doing up and around. You have had a terrible, brutal shock, but you are not badly injured physically. Is that clear?''

Caroline nodded. ''I can walk and converse but not necessarily remain sensible for any length of time. Good, that should serve to cover a multitude of sins.''

Rogers nodded. ''It's been good to be among friends of the Union and of freedom. And to be doctor to someone who stands a chance of getting better. But I really must be back to my unit.''

He bowed solemnly to all of them, and was gone.

It was early afternoon now, and time to be going. According to Ma, they'd had two brief visits from Confederate cavalry the night before, nothing particularly serious, but just what you would expect whenever there was a fugitive loose in the area. Nevertheless, patrolling units were likely to be in the area, including very possibly the cavalry troop they had encountered the day before, so it seemed a good idea to travel inconspicuously. One of her grown sons, a quiet man named Joe, had been using the wagon and mule for a long time to run local people into town, as well as to go there for marketing, and anyone riding on Joe's wagon was likely not to get a second glance. Besides, it meant Juky could try to sleep in the back of the lurching contraption, and that could at least be no worse for him than trying to walk the remaining six miles to Richmond.

After all the chaos so far on the mission, it was a great relief that the journey into Richmond itself was eventless. Joe wasn't given to conversation, Strang was normally silent—now *that* was different from Matt

Perney!—and Samson was too interested in his surroundings to talk much other than to ask the occasional question, although usually he could find what
he wanted in Prescott Heller's memories.

That left the burden of conversation on Caroline,
who was remarkably well able to bear it. Samson
mentally swatted himself for noting that in this she was
very like Sarah. She talked about plays she'd seen at
"The Theater"—that seemed to be all the name it
had—at Broad and Seventy, and books she'd read,
about art and politics, about everything and anything, always managing to draw Strang and Samson
into it, although it was pretty clear that Strang thought
the girl was just plain silly.

When the name Karl Marx came up, Samson was
startled enough to sit up straight for a moment. "Oh,
do you know his writing, Mr. Toole?"

"Uh, a little bit about it," Samson said.

"Well, I think he's quite the best reporter the New
York *Trib*'s ever had, and it was sheer foolishness of
them to lose him."

Samson's head whirled for a second, but then he
realized that Prescott Heller had indeed read some of
Marx's news reporting in the *Tribune,* that it really was
the same one and that Marx was notable mostly for
being radically pro-Union and for having a much better grasp of military strategy than most reporters.

After all the traveling in time, to find a name that
was still important in his own time was almost like
recognizing an old friend.

Finally the Richmond Turnpike carried them into the city. They passed through the Interior Line, a long row of connected fortifications and entrenchments that seemed to trigger a memory in Samson....

Gas attack! Shells were roaring overhead and everywhere men were groping desperately for the life-saving masks. Boche machine-gun rounds were whining just overhead, and that meant very likely the Germans were coming over the top. Samson leapt to man a .50-caliber—

That was it, of course. He might have realized that since Jackson Houston had been born in 1919, he must have died...1919? Hadn't the war been over? Well, that was a question for another day.

Anyway, one thing was plain. He'd been to World War I in his long line of reincarnations, so he would have to expect to go back sooner or later. The sight of the fortifications here—so similar to what had stretched across France fifty years later—had reminded him. But time enough to fight that one when he got there....

The day was hot and humid, and now that it was the very hottest part of late afternoon even Caroline was drooping. But she seemed to force herself to perk up and say, "This part coming is not really Richmond yet. It's Manchester, across the river. We'll be coming in where the turnpike becomes Hull Street, and then going over Mayo's Bridge."

In the past half hour, quite a bit of traffic had accumulated on the turnpike, and Samson noted that another big difference from the twentieth century was that since there was no engine noise and the wagons and carts were open, you couldn't count on a conversation staying private when you were traveling. Ever since other wagons had shown up, he and Jim and Caroline had had to be very careful to keep the conversation to safe topics and to stay in their assumed characters.

Mayo's Bridge was a wide plank bridge, big enough to carry carriage traffic in both directions, supported by stone pillars to a point about halfway to the middle of the James River, and then by wooden pilings after that. The military part of Samson's mind noted that it was the only road—as opposed to rail—bridge, and that though it might be work to get its seasoned timbers on fire, the people of the city would be cut off without anywhere to flee quickly if it burned.

Luckily it will hold up until most people who need to flee have done so, a year from now, Master Xi reassured him.

The Mayo Bridge connected with Fifteenth Street on the Richmond side, a busy commercial district where the tobacco warehouses tended to cluster. Pointing at one of them emphatically, Caroline said, "You know what my daddy told me they have in there? He said it used to be a factory where they processed tobacco, and now it's where they ought to process more hemp if the President had a spine."

It took Samson a moment to realize what she was saying. Once again his twentieth-century memories had gotten in his way, and besides, he had almost remembered whatever it was that he had been trying to all day.

"Prison, I reckon." Jim Strang's drawl sounded as if it were just barely worth the effort to make the conversation.

"Yep. That's Castle Thunder, where they keep the traitors and the deserters." She pointed upriver. "And that up there's Belle Isle where they keep the Yankee prisoners, and down there's the old Libby Brothers' Ships' Chandlery, that they've made into a prison to hold Yankee officers. Ever since the war, we are just filling up with prisons in this city. I don't think that's quite nice." She continued to prattle idiotically. It was annoying, but not as annoying as it would have been if it hadn't been an act. The biggest problem was that even though the warm afternoon sun and the gentle rocking of the wagon was putting Samson to sleep, he had to stay alert in case she dropped other important information into the conversation.

The Exchange Hotel had been elegant once, and it really just needed some repairs and replacements that were hard to come by in wartime to be so again. It still was expensive, even by inflated Confederate standards, but since part of the mission for anyone who worked for Lafayette Baker was always to pass off as much counterfeit Confederate money as possible, there was no problem with staying there. The "modern" facilities included a small separate slave quarters, to which Juky went without saying much. It looked as though his mouth must be hurting him badly. There was also a conveniently situated bathroom down the hall that consisted of a tub, with hot water having to be ordered up from downstairs for a fee that staggered the imagination, plus an open standpipe for dumping the chamber pot down, thus sparing the guests from having to either hurl the muck from their windows or carry it out to dump in the gutter. The pipe itself opened into the storm sewers below. Samson hoped he wouldn't have to be around that when it rained.

For right now, however, he was quite sure that he wasn't going to mind a bit. The thought of a night without interruptions, between clean sheets, was wonderful, and here at Fifteenth and Franklin, they were no more than a half dozen city blocks from Castle Thunder itself. After a not very good dinner with Caroline and Jim, he got into his bed fairly happily. At least he was in place up-class enough not to have a lot of bedbugs.

HE AWOKE when a hand touched his forehead. In the bright light from the gaslights on Franklin, he could see that it was Caroline, standing there in her night-gown. "What?" he asked.

"Your friend Jim Strang is no gentleman," she said. "May I sit?"

He sat up, blinking, and said, "Uh, sure. Would you care to be more specific about Jim's failings?"

"Well, last night after you went to sleep, while he was on guard, I couldn't sleep so I sat down next to him to talk to him. He . . . oh, it was disgraceful."

"He tried to kiss you."

"Well, yes. And succeeded. That was all right, actually. But then with no invitation at all—I certainly did not ask him to—well, Mr. Toole, he . . ."

Samson had been mildly amused up till now, but he was beginning to wonder just what had happened, and irrational as it was, he didn't like the guy who was going to be his best friend in three more lifetimes coming on to the girl he was going to marry, even if that was one hundred fifteen years in the future. "What did he do?" he whispered gently. "It's okay, it's not your fault, and I'm not going to start a fight with him about it. Tell me if it helps."

She sniffled. "Now I feel very foolish. He fondled my bosom, Mr. Toole. And I'm afraid I . . . well, I enjoyed it. So twice, so far tonight, he's been knocking at my door, wanting to come in. . . ."

Well, Samson had to admit, this wouldn't have been completely out of character for Matt Perney, bearing in mind that Samson wasn't married to this girl, no matter what he felt.

"So, er, what can I do for you?"

She sighed. "I thought that if I came down here, he would at least decide that I preferred you, and because he has some vestige of honor, he will probably leave me alone. But I would not make trouble between you and your friend."

"No, that's okay," Samson said, "but we both need sleep, and there's only one bed here."

"If I were to join you in yours, would your conduct be honorable?"

"As long as yours is," he said, grinning at her.

"Humph." The answer seemed satisfactory. She got into the bed next to him. The huge old pillow was large enough for both heads if she lay close to him, and Samson wasn't displeased that she was willing to.

She whispered to him, "Now, you know that you have it completely in your power to destroy my reputation."

"Never," he said. "Just make sure you get back to your own room before there's too many people up and about."

She snuggled closer and very timidly took his hand. He decided to try a brotherly kiss on the forehead, and she tilted her mouth up to meet his. It didn't come out particularly brotherly.

As the kiss broke, he realized she was trembling.

"It's okay," he said. "We won't do anything you don't want to do." His heart was pounding like a runaway engine. Jeez, he'd forgotten what it was like to be a teenager.

"Exactly what I'm afraid of," she whispered back, and took him into her arms, pressing her body to his. "At least tell me you love me."

"I do. More than you can imagine," he said. "You might say we were meant for each other."

They kissed, long and tenderly. After that she didn't resist anything, and seemed eager to be shown how to do things, until finally he gently drew her nightgown off her and pressed her legs apart. "You know that this, uh..."

"Could get me with child, Mr. Toole?"

"At least call me Sean," he said. "And a few very close friends back home always called me Daniel." He stroked her gently but steadily, getting her ready, and kissed her stiff nipples.

"Daniel," she whispered, "we aren't going to live through this mission, are we?"

"It doesn't look good," he whispered back, "but we're still at large, and we've got a chance. And if we both live, I am going to propose, believe me or not."

"I trust you with anything," she said, and pulled his face up to kiss her again. When he entered her, he was slow and careful, trying to make sure she wasn't hurt, but things took on a rhythm of their own, and when they were finished there was a little blood and she needed to wash with water from the basin. "I think I'll be sore in the morning," she said. "Oh, I want to *live*, Daniel, even if I have to endure some shame, and I warn you that if you don't propose I shall just simply have to haunt you till you do."

She cuddled against him, still naked, her cool, moist back to him, holding one of his big arms against her tiny body as if it were a teddy bear. He thought he might lie awake till morning looking at her red hair in the gaslight coming in through the window, but really he fell asleep and slept as well as he had at any time since he'd started his journey through time.

4

As the dawn came up, she kissed him and slipped out of the room, sneaking back down the hall after a quick exchange of I-love-yous.

Master Xi, Samson thought as he snuggled into the warm hollow in the mattress where she had been, still smelling the mixture of oil and perfume from her hair on the pillow, *this seems like a pretty odd penance.*

What you are doing is not penance, Master Xi said. *You are to make things right—how much you suffer doing so is not relevant. But there will be pain enough, soon enough. You have been a soldier for a very long time, in many generations. Surely you have learned that when pleasure comes your way, it is to be enjoyed today, and not to be hoarded up as if it were gold and you a miser.*

Samson nodded and fell back asleep. An hour and a half later the knocking of one of the house slaves woke him up.

At breakfast, down in one of the little private dining rooms, Caroline got a short chance, as Strang went to get them more corn bread, to whisper in Samson's ear, "He's apologized twice for not being a gentleman last night, and I do believe he was asleep before I came to your room.''

''How are you?'' he murmured back.

''Sore. And in love, Daniel.''

They exchanged smiles so warm that Samson thought the butter on the table must be melting.

More than the day before, Samson was desperately trying to remember that ''something important'' that wouldn't come to him. He began to have a horrible, sinking feeling that it was something Prescott Heller was able to keep from him. . . .

The Heller part of his mind was very quiet this morning, however. Well, after all, the kid had lost his virginity the night before, and in a really tender, loving way. That tended to make you a little quiet and shy afterward, or at least it had been that way for Samson in all the previous lives he had access to. It beat the hell out of raping some poor kid, he thought at Heller, and felt the boy's anger flare within him. The contrast, obviously, was exactly what was bothering this lifetime's version of himself.

That and the fact that Prescott Heller, too, like it or not, was in love with Caroline Carelias.

Samson smiled. It wasn't as if it were a disease, or was going to hurt him.

Among the skills they had picked up in Baker's Secret Service, Jim Strang had revealed an unexpected talent for forgery and counterfeiting. So he carefully drew up appropriate papers in the little private parlor that morning, basing them loosely on the documents they had had back when they'd been impersonating

Confederate officers. Juky had been permitted to join them after they finished eating. He said he felt much better, though his speech was still a little indistinct from his freshly sewn split lip.

As Strang drew, Samson could feel Heller's presence in his mind like an itchy spot under his clothing. Whatever was being hidden, it was becoming a real battle of wills between the two of them.

Finally, when Strang's copies of the orders met his own exacting standards, he sprinkled the fine white sand over them to help the ink dry before he would acid-treat them to make them look roadworn. "Maybe I should see about gettin' y'all a cab. It might look better to arrive like that, sirs," Juky said. "Cabstand is right out this window, and—" He pulled back the curtain for an instant, froze like a terrified rabbit and let the curtain fall back into place.

"What is it?" Samson asked. He seemed to feel adrenaline dump into his bloodstream like a hot-water faucet thrown wide open.

"Paddy rollers. Never seen so many in my life," Juky said, low and quiet, but now perfectly calm. "Five across the street pretending to loiter. Three driving cabs. Two watching from a rooftop with rifles. And more I didn't see, I'm sure."

Paddy rollers. Underground Railroad slang for detectives. No one wasted any time asking Juky if he was sure. If he didn't have a perfect nose for detectives, he would never have lived this long.

"Hope y'all came armed to breakfast," Juky said, " 'cause I don't think we can go back to the rooms."

Quietly he drew his revolver from its concealed pocket in his trousers.

The rifles had been concealed, broken down in the luggage, but both the men had their Colt repeaters and Caroline had her dueling pistols.

"Only one exit from this room," Samson said very quietly. "I suggest whatever we do, we don't go through it. At least we're on the ground floor. What's it look like from the window on the other wall?"

Juky walked around and casually brushed the curtain aside for a moment, glancing out as if bored. "Not good. Count at least four paddy rollers in the windows, probably already sighted in on the window."

Samson's guess was that they had less than a minute before the knock would come at the door. This had all the marks of one of General Alexander's operations: everything done in depth to make sure that there would be no escape.

"Window by the cabs, then, and figure we might have to take one of them as a hostage," Samson said. "Can we bust it out? Any bars or anything?"

"Nothing that can't be coped with," Juky said. "One of you big men best go first. Let me hold 'em here. Then one of you can hand Miss Caroline to the one outside, and then the last two can come after."

They both nodded. Strang smiled and said, "I think I'm a bit smaller than you, and better suited to window jumping. I'll go out first."

Samson nodded. In moments he, Caroline and Strang were at the window, and Juky was by the door.

With a big swing, Samson raised a chair over his head and bashed the window out. An instant later Jim Strang had sprung through. A rifle slug pocked the floor in front of Samson, and then Strang's Colt was blazing defiance. For good measure, Samson hurled chairs through the two other windows, drawing fire to those, then swung Caroline up and over the sill. Strang caught her lightly, and then both of them hit the ground.

As Samson turned back to cover Juky's retreat, he heard one of Caroline's dueling pistols bark behind him, and another shot, high and erratic, shattered the upper pane on the window, spraying glass onto the floor.

Juky had gotten the drop on the men getting ready to rush the door, and they were well back. With a parting shot, Juky bounced back next to Samson, and the two of them dived through the window together, not knowing what they would find.

They dropped into crouches on opposite sides of the window. A fusillade of wild shots spattered the side of the building, but nothing came close to them. One glance showed Samson that Caroline was already in one of the cabs, on the front seat, her remaining pistol at the head of the terrified detective who had been posing as a cabbie. A glimpse of a passenger told him that Strang was aboard, as well.

Samson and Juky charged forward almost as one man, Juky whirling to fire one shot through the window through which they had come. A shriek from inside told them that Juky had guessed right—someone had gotten overexcited and rushed forward too soon.

The instant Samson and Juky were in the cab, Caroline shouted "drive" at the detective, and they were rocketing east on Franklin, toward the Capitol. Afraid of hitting their own man, the Confederate agents didn't fire. Juky and Samson reloaded hastily, and Juky turned around to put a couple of shots into the dirt behind them to slow up any pursuit.

Their luck seemed to be holding, at least until the driver suddenly fell sideways, letting himself roll off limply into the street, leaving the cab temporarily driverless, the wildly galloping horses headed for the state courthouse in the Capitol Mall with no one holding the reins. But that lasted only a moment. An instant later Caroline had the reins and, shouting and struggling with the horses, got them turned twice so that they were now roaring up Bank Street.

A part of the back of Samson's brain noted that if they got away at all, it would be literally past the windows of the Confederate Secret Service.

He turned to speak to Jim Strang and for the first time saw the blood oozing onto the seat from his friend's shattered left shoulder. Strang's eyes were open and he was clearly conscious, but there was a lot of blood, and it was clear that the back part of his shoulder must be torn to ribbons. God, why couldn't it just be like the movies, where the shoulder was never serious? There were major blood vessels in there, and from the way Strang looked, Samson guessed that he was in real danger of bleeding to death.

An instant later Samson was pushing his clean handkerchief against the bloody exit wound, the heel of his hand holding it down as hard as he could. Strang groaned at the pressure and at the rough, jouncing ride Caroline was giving them. "I don't think that's a leak you can plug, old son. I can feel it getting pretty sleepy right now, and I don't think I've got a lot of time. That's quite a gal. Don't let her drive like that if you marry her."

His half smile almost made Samson feel better. If nothing else, Strang still knew where he was and why the world was bouncing, shaking and veering wildly. But then Strang's eyes rolled up into his head, and Samson redoubled his efforts to get the pressure, through the already saturated handkerchief, to stop the bleeding.

Behind them, meanwhile, a few detectives had managed to get horses and were rapidly gaining. Juky opened up on them, but between the bouncing of the cab and the generally low accuracy of the pistol, he only managed to slow them down a little, making them keep their distance.

Desperately trying to keep his sodden handkerchief pressed to Strang's wound, Samson also braced up to fire at them.

At that moment Caroline took a hard left onto Eighth Street, throwing Samson against Strang and nearly flinging them over. Samson's shot went wild, screaming off brickwork. The cab slewed wildly, but she kept pressing and brought them into a small alley, then around a hard right turn to another one, and finally out onto Main Street, headed the other way at a more sedate pace. "Juky! Up here and make it look like you belong here!"

Pocketing his pistol, he was up there in an instant. "Where to?" he said, quietly.

"Anyplace we can pull up for even a few minutes. Right now they're still looking for a cab being driven much too fast by a red-haired woman. If we can get rid of the cab and perhaps split up..."

Juky nodded. "I'm going to head us back over toward Manchester for the time being. Chances are they'll look for us in the city for a while before they check the bridges." He kept his voice low.

Samson heard all this while he was tending to Strang, but he had little time to comment on it. The man was breathing hard and fast, a good sign in some ways, but he was still unconscious and, judging by the dark blood oozing from the wound, he was probably bleeding internally. They badly needed a doctor. Maybe Juky could find one from the Railroad? It seemed likely that all of them were now marked and there would be little chance for anyone to go out on the streets unobtrusively.

As they approached Mayo's Bridge, Juky saw the Confederate pickets out and tried to nonchalantly continue on Main. It seemed almost to work, since they had gotten past the guards, when one of them shouted and started to run after them. Since there were just three guards, and only this one was close, Samson shot the one approaching, hitting him in the gut, putting him on the ground screaming in agony. Juky whipped up the tired cab horses as Samson took another shot at the now-pursuing guards.

One of them passed, raised a rifle and fired. Beside him on the cab seat, Samson heard Strang make a noise like a grunted cough, and when he looked, he saw that the shot had taken him full in the middle of the back, probably right through the heart. Jim Strang was dead.

Juky, having finally gotten some distance on the guards, was pulling into the complex alleyways that led among the warehouses. In a moment he had found a building standing vacant, probably waiting a shipment for later that day, and they were under cover.

Less than half an hour ago they had been having breakfast at the Exchange. Now Jim was dead, and the odds weren't good that any of the rest of them would see sunset. Gently Juky and Samson carried the body into one of the smaller storerooms and set it down on a bench. Drawing pencil and paper from his pocket, Samson wrote "James Strang, lieutenant, First Missouri Volunteers" and tucked it under his dead friend's collar.

He wanted to tell himself, there in the dusty warehouse, that this didn't really matter, that Strang would be born again as Matt Perney, had been born many times. But all he could think of was Jim Strang going into the Wind Between Time frightened and alone and still unable to make the final crossing. He looked down at the dead face of his friend and wept. Neither Caroline nor Juky disturbed him.

Outside he heard them give the cab horses a hard slap on the flank to get them in motion. The horses would probably walk for a few blocks before they realized no one was asking them to, or they might even decide that they knew their way home to their stables. In either case, they would at least not be around here to point out the fugitives.

Oh, God, Matt—Jim—whatever his True Name was, why did he have to be dead? In his two adventures before this, Samson had spent seemingly ages of time getting to know and like the stranger that he had known by the names of Turenne and Bastida in different times, but he had had so little time with this friend. . . .

And tell me, Master Xi said in his mind, *what would be enough time with a good friend? Enough time so that at the end of it you could say, this was a good friend and I have loved him dearly and now I am done with him and don't need to see him again?*

Point taken, Samson thought, but oh—

Your destinies are bound together. You will see each other again, Master Xi said. *And if you are already wondering what his True Name might be, you are well along the road. Grieve for a friend's pain and for your separation, but never say goodbye forever.*

Samson looked down at the body, though it wasn't an easy thing to consider, and sighed. A hand touched his shoulder.

It was Juky. "You know we will have to leave him here?"

"I've already tagged him," Samson said, gesturing at the strip of paper he had shoved into Strang's collar. "At least his name will go on the lists and across the lines, and his folks will hear something." He sighed. "He wasn't religious at all. I guess there's not much need to say any words over him. Wouldn't seem in keeping."

As they turned away, Caroline was just coming in. She walked over to Strang and looked at him for a long time, then lightly brushed his untidy hair away from one eye and gently pressed the eyes closed.

In the next room, grimly they sat down to confer.

"Well," Juky said, "for what it's worth, we are within five blocks of Castle Thunder. And it's going to be mighty tough getting out of Richmond at all. I guess we might as well try escaping with prisoners as without, if you still want to."

Samson shrugged. The others might have noticed a faraway look in his eyes and thought that he was grieving for Jim Strang, and let him be for a moment because of that. He was grieving, but that wasn't what had occupied his mind. Like a glimpse caught out of the corner of one eye, he had sensed what the forgotten thing was, and now he knew for sure that Prescott Heller held it in his section of the mind.

With absolute firmness, Samson pressed Heller's mind back and...*squeezed* it, as the only word Dan could think of. He pushed harder, felt Heller struggle and squirm and begin to suffer real pain.

And then he knew, and his pain was worse than anything Heller had experienced by far.

Prescott Heller had had a secret communication channel out of the Baker organization and had been reporting regularly. Everything about the mission—its membership, goal, methods, timing, date—everything had been in his messages to Maury at the Submarine Battery Service.

The Rebs had known where to place a torpedo to blow the *Commodore Jones* and her crew of seventy out of existence. They had known where and when to send the first cavalry squad—hell, now that he thought about it, the cavalry had arrived with nooses pre-tied. If Juky hadn't guided the party off the main road and thus made the Confederates lose the trail during the time they were at Ma's Underground Railroad station, all of them—except Heller himself, and perhaps Caroline—would long ago have been hanged.

Even now, the Confederates knew enough to look for two tall men together, a black man with a bashed-up face and a red-haired girl of sixteen. There might be an occasional mistaken identity with that description, but every group that looked like that was bound to be stopped.

Well, they no longer quite looked like that. One of the tall men wouldn't be traveling with them anymore.

But the overwhelming, sickening feeling in his stomach still wouldn't leave him alone. Strang, Eilemann and the major were all dead due to Prescott Heller's treachery.

Coldly, but with all the dignity he could muster, the boy's voice in Samson's brain reminded Samson who was being faithful to his original mission and who was not.

Daniel Samson's head ached with the knowledge, and tears ran down his face. When he looked at his two surviving friends, they were both leaning forward, obviously worried, wondering if he would be all right.

He dragged a rough, dirty sleeve over his face, feeling the tears streak the grit there, and said, "I'm all right. Really I am. But I've just realized that there is a way for me to get us into Castle Thunder and out with the prisoners. It's something I had better do alone and then meet up with you later. And it seems to me that by now tall men, injured Negros and red-haired women—especially together—are probably drawing a lot of attention."

Juky nodded. "If you think you know a way, you're a long way ahead of me. I can always slip down to the waterfront from here and join the freedmen's line for longshore work. Nobody'll care if I stand in that line for hours, and nobody'll look for me there. 'Course I won't get any work, either, not this late in the day, but that's not what I'm going for."

Caroline nodded. "I think with a shawl—and I've got one—I can do a fair job of getting to somewhere else. You're going to be the hard one to hide, Sean."

The tiny smile Juky flashed him at hearing this very proper girl address him by his first name, gave Samson a little welling of warmth in his stomach, despite the terrible things that had happened and the dangers he could feel rising.

"You tend to learn how to hide what you are in this business," he said. "So I know a lot more about hiding height than you or Juky do, just as I suspect neither Juky nor I know much about how to hide being a young red-haired woman. And neither of us, Caroline, knows anything about hiding a Negro in the South."

"Sense in that," Juky agreed. "Okay, when and where do we meet again?"

That part was easy enough to settle. It was the leaving the warehouse that was difficult, and not for fear of being watched. Juky walked out with an empty barrel on his shoulder, making him virtually invisible to any white man passing. A few minutes later, after a hard hug and kiss, Caroline, shawl pulled over her head, shoes and stockings removed, hooped crinoline thrown away and dress torn to be walkable in, wandered out, a sort of witless stare on her face that suggested she was one more destitute beggar of the many now roaming Richmond's streets.

That left Samson a few minutes to wait. He thought of saying goodbye one more time to Jim Strang, but he had already done that, and besides, the dead thing in the next room wasn't really his friend anymore.

When he left, he just walked straight out, up the middle of the street, and headed toward the Capitol, letting Prescott Heller's memories show him the way. He knew exactly where he was going—to Captain Maury's office at the Submarine Battery Service.

If this worked, they would have a way to pull it off. And if it didn't, well, then at least Samson would be the only one of them whom he personally sent to the gallows.

The whole way, Prescott Heller screamed and gibbered in his mind, feeling what it was that Samson planned. The shrieks of pain and the occasional headaches Heller sent were the main things Dan had to take his mind off the recent tragedies and the dangers yet to come, so they were not unwelcome.

5

The building at Ninth and Bank was what one would expect the headquarters of an Intelligence service to be. That is, it was bland and inconspicuous, but if Dan thought about it he could see that there were very few ways to rush the building directly and lots of ways to enter or leave without being seen. It was as familiar to Prescott Heller as the dorms at VMI or his own bedroom at home.

In fact, Samson realized, much more familiar than his own bedroom at home. One of Heller's ugly little secrets was that he had certainly been sent away from home a lot as a kid. Not so much because his parents didn't like him, but because the plantation, once good overseers were procured, could look after itself for large parts of the year. His mother and father had preferred to spend their time socializing in Richmond or Charleston, socializing in a way that emphatically didn't have a role for a small boy. So it had been off to boarding schools almost from the first.

Heller resented this picking of his memories. His idealized pictures of his mother and father didn't stand up well to what Samson extracted about them. The father was shallow, not bright, a first-rate salesman and money-grubber who had bought his way into local society. And the mother—

Heller shrieked at that one, but it was clear enough. "Dear Mother's" family were tobacco, not cotton, but their land was played out, and what they had going for them was only that they were a cadet branch of an old Virginia line, good at being pretty and filling out a party roster, useless for anything but leisure, gossip... and adultery.

Heller did everything a part of the mind with no ability to command the physical can do. It was a great raging tantrum Samson could feel inside, a tantrum about the things that a child should not have to know.

For the first time he almost felt sorry for the little turd. No wonder he had fallen so hard for the duty-and-honor ethic of VMI—hell, the duty-and-honor part of it was good and decent and true. The fact that it had gotten bound up with not just slavery but with despising poor whites, and hating any of his fellow Americans who were not of his own region and class, was a tragedy for Heller as much as for anyone else. Capable of great courage, he was bright and articulate, the kind of person who might have made a valuable citizen and soldier despite his bad beginnings, if the people in charge of raising him had not themselves been contaminated with racism and hatred.

He was shocked to feel a little touch of pleasure coming up from Prescott Heller at that moment. He wouldn't have thought that being appreciated by Daniel Samson could have made the young Southern aristocrat feel any happiness.

There was a moment of embarrassment between them. Samson's foot hesitated on the doorsill of Bank and Ninth. It was really very simple. Often with nothing else to do, trapped inside his own body, Prescott Heller had picked through Samson's memories and, little though he might like Samson's values, had seen Samson's other wars, experienced his courage and skills, and had come to admire him.

Daniel Samson shook his head. He had never exactly thought he might end up as a positive influence on youth, especially not when the youth was himself.

When he entered, there was a tiny one-armed man, about forty years old, behind the huge desk. Reynolds had been too short to enlist, but he'd managed to find a doctor who had the appropriate problems with reading a yardstick, and had left his arm at Shiloh. As the younger brother of one of Jefferson Davis's old West Point cronies, he'd gotten out of the hospital and into this job with little trouble.

"Prescott Heller?" Reynolds asked incredulously.

"Reckon you heard I was in the city," Samson said, trying to manage a little bit of the expected adolescent swagger, even though it was the last thing he was likely to feel.

"Other than a gun battle three blocks from the Capitol, a stolen taxicab, and three men in there shouting at each other right now about whether or not you've turned your coat, Pres, no, I hadn't a clue. I would figure they'd probably want to talk to you, but I'd also figure that they'd insist I pat you down for hardware. Hope you don't mind—and if you're going to bash me over the head and barge in there and kill somebody, I'd sure appreciate it if you'd make a neat job of it, 'cause I sure would rather believe you're loyal.''

An instant of explanation flashed through Samson's mind. Reynolds had helped to send far too many boys not yet out of their teens to their deaths, and many of them had come out of VMI, and he had suffered for everyone of them as if it were his own son. Samson grinned, raised his arms and stood in the middle of the space in front of the desk while Reynolds got down from his stool and came around.

"Might damned well need a stepladder for you, there, Cay-det," the older man said. "Let's start in your boots and work up."

He'd had time, sitting there in Ma's concealed cellar, to do some sewing, and so he'd been able to transfer everything from his Confederate uniform to these civilian clothes. His boots yielded two bowie knives and a small folding straight razor. A concealed pocket in a pant leg turned up another short blade. The Colt in his belt, the throwing knife in the inside pocket of the coat under the collar along the spine, and the derringer in the inside flat pocket of the coat completed the arsenal. Samson had to admit complete admiration. Reynolds had found it all on one pass, though he promptly made another trip over Samson's body to make sure.

"Well, guess that's it. Okay, if you want to go on in, I suppose the worst you can do is try to bite the captain to death. He's in his big office, second floor, back room. Figure you know where that is." Reynolds quietly dusted Samson's coat and pulled it straight. "You be careful, and you know enough to just tell Captain Maury the truth, I reckon. Because he'll get whatever's really going on, no matter what you say."

Somehow Samson doubted that.

The building must have been a bank or a counting house before the war, for all the woodwork was expensive and elaborate. The mahogany balustrade wound up the side of a flight of steep stairs, and it was oiled and polished till it glowed, most likely by Reynolds, Samson thought. His fingers drifted along the smooth dustless perfection as he went up the stairs. He was reading through Heller's memories of the first terrifying time he had come here, not knowing what it could be about and half suspecting that his father had pulled strings to keep him out of combat in some pointless backwater bureau.

Should have known better than that, Heller commented. He probably hasn't bothered to learn anything other than my rank and theater. In Charleston, having "my boy, a first lieutenant up in Virginia," was good enough for impressing the fluttery young things off the plantations, and that would be all his father would be interested in.

Samson's boots echoed with heavy thumps on the dark, gleaming hardwood floor. The spring sun shone in through a window at the end of the corridor. How many times had he taken this walk, back before Gettysburg and before he had been sent across the lines?

And what had become of the other young men who used to come up here with him? How many caught by Union troops and summarily hanged, how many under questioning by Lafayette Baker in the old Capitol Prison, how many still out there, in military units or in the great Northern cities, quietly going about their assigned duties without a comrade or a real friend, for months on end with no orders or contact from this office? It had all seemed so simple, and so romantic and adventurous, back in the first years of the war.

The thought brought back the memory of Jim Strang, dead not quite three hours... and to Samson's mild surprise and pleasure, Prescott Heller, too, felt some sadness at that death. *I reckon I can be sorry for any brave man dead, without having to love Yankees,* Heller thought at him.

The door was thick and heavy. It wasn't a building where things ought to be overheard. Samson knocked on it firmly, and in a moment it opened.

Captain Matthew Fontaine Maury, before the war, had been the nearest thing that the United States Navy had had to a chief scientist. It was said that if anything at all was known of the oceans, it was known by Maury. If the war hadn't come, no doubt he would have been happy to spend the rest of his life patiently hooking fact to fact, observation to observation, to slowly build up the theory from which a real science of the oceans could grow. Even now, if a visitor came to his office unexpectedly during one of the rare breaks Maury permitted himself, he was as likely to find the captain poring over a set of drawings of mollusks or over Darwin's *Voyage of the HMS Beagle,* as over anything military.

But as a loyal Virginian, he had turned the same powerful mind that had penetrated so far into the black depths of the ocean to the more difficult task of penetrating the minds of his adversaries. He was a slim man, balding, with wild hair around the fringes of his head that wouldn't stay combed under any circumstances, wide-set intelligent eyes and a nose that looked as if someone had set out to flatten it with a hammer and then given up the job as too difficult.

If he was surprised to see Prescott Heller, the reaction was too brief for Samson to see.

"Come in," he said. "I do believe you are the very person who can resolve our riddles here."

There were two other men in the room. One of them Samson recognized immediately from Heller's memories. The wide-set sensitive brown eyes, fine-boned features, neatly trimmed thick black beard and high forehead—an effect that men on both sides said made him resemble Satan—was unmistakable. It was General Edward Porter Alexander, head of the Confederate Signal Corps, most of which was the War Department Secret Service, the Confederacy's equivalent of the DIA.

The other man was tall and distinguished, somebody Hollywood would have cast to play the President in a political thriller if Gregory Peck weren't available. His piercing eyes shot a glance of keen intelligence from under heavy brows. His forehead was wide and high, his face gaunt with tiredness, and the jaunty little beard that clung to the underside of his chin was much whiter than the last time that Heller had seen it, a couple of years ago when he had served as an honor guard at a public speech.

It took him a moment to recognize the man only because it seemed inconceivable that he would be taking his valuable time to be here over a matter that seemed as small, even to Samson, as Prescott Heller. But there was no mistake. It was Jefferson Davis, the President of the Confederacy.

"This is the young officer we've been discussing," Maury said mildly. "You will note he has arrived here under his own power."

"And was it also under his own power that he shot two of my men early this morning?" Porter asked.

"Not *my* shots, sir. And the man who fired those shots is dead in a warehouse down by the waterfront." He told them where.

Alexander made hasty notes, then said, "Excuse me, of course?" He rang the bell that brought Reynolds upstairs to get the order for next door. "In twenty minutes or so we will have at least that much confirmed. Now, what the hell have you been doing, Lieutenant?"

It was the most reasonable question anyone had asked Samson in a long time. "Well, sir." he began, and told the story from the beginning, with only two changes. First of all, any violence that had to be explained he made into Strang's doing. "The man was strong as an ox and brave as a lion, sir, though like most of these Missouri frontiersmen, he wasn't near as smart as either. They started to search him and—wham!—he had two of them down and had shot two more. I had been just about to reveal myself to them. If I'd already done so, you'd have had another corpse at that bridge, I'm sure, for I know I could never have gotten the drop on Strang. The man was brave and lucky, but fortunately he ran out of luck this morning."

Secondly, he described himself and Caroline being blindfolded before being taken in to the Underground Railroad station, but the description he supplied was really of a ruined cabin that he knew the Union had stopped using as a drop point, over on the other side of the Richmond and Petersburg Railroad. If they went to close it down, they would find signs enough of people, but chances were they wouldn't find anybody or anything of importance.

He just hoped no squatters had moved in.

"So you stayed with them to see what more you could learn. Well, there's a certain sense in that, but where are the girl and the Negro now?" Maury asked him.

"I am to meet with them again this afternoon. It was about that that I wanted to talk with you. I think this fish is not completely played out, sir. If we can play it right—"

President Davis cleared his throat, and the room instantly fell silent. "I begin to see some sense in this operation, but I would have to tell you, Maury, that this is the very *most* initiative I ever want to see from one of your agents. I should say we are coming out

well ahead from it—at least the traitors in Castle
Thunder are remaining there, and we've caused Abe
Lincoln to expend some of his best agents to no purpose at all." He combed his tiny goatee with his fingers. "On the other hand, I cannot imagine what
further value can be gained. I'm quite satisfied that
this young man is loyal, but for the love of God, sir,
given the uproar he's caused, let us simply arrest and
hang the Negro, jail the girl and put this young man in
charge of an infantry company somewhere. Richmond is a nervous enough city right now, with Butler
advancing on our south and very little between him
and us, without having shots traded within the hearing of my Senate. I have enough trouble with them as
it is."

Captain Maury listened patiently and watched as
Jefferson Davis sat down on the windowsill, stretching out his long, long legs and turning to stare out the
window. Maury had been at West Point with Davis,
Samson remembered, and seemed to know how to get
more out of him than almost anyone else. After a long
pause, the scientist spoke. "Sir, we need to wring every
bit of advantage we can out of everything that comes
our way. I would like to hear what Lieutenant Heller
has in mind first, before we give him orders. If we
don't care for it, we can always give him the orders we
would have originally."

General Alexander shrugged. "Damn it, Matt, why
is it you always sound so reasonable? All right, let's
hear what more he thinks we can do."

"Well," Samson said, "if you recall two of my dispatches, Captain, I did note that once those Peace Society men were out of Castle Thunder and across the James, the Union's problem would be just beginning. They won't have one bit of respect if they come in with the bluecoats or on a Yankee gunboat. What they have to do is make their way home and get themselves reestablished as the prominent citizens they once were in their home communities, if their disloyalty is going to be put to any use by the Yankees. It's one thing, in an area where the war and the Confederate government have never been popular anyway, for the local newspaper editor or the former mayor to have broken out of jail and be organizing a secret society of local citizens to seize power and surrender the area to federal troops. Bless our independent Southern spirits, that feels like local people deciding a local matter. It would be quite another thing for that same man to come in after Yankee troops overrun the area, and appear to be working for them, because little as they like us, they don't have much use for Yankees up in the hills, either.

"So the Union plan always had to turn on getting these men back home *through the Confederacy,* and the only organization that could do that, sir, is the Railroad."

Alexander was nodding grudgingly. "I begin to see where you're going, Lieutenant, and I see some value in it. Since the war came and slaves have found so many other ways of escaping, the Railroad has been the main means of communication for treasonable

organizations throughout the South. Little as we like
to remember it, the bulk of Underground Railroad
operations were always conducted by white Southerners. The Negroes and the Yankee abolitionists would
have been powerless without the help of so many people down here who ought to know better. And many
of those people, claiming some damned nonsense or
other about 'loyalty' to the Union, are still out there,
moving deserters back home and messages between
our disloyal people.''

"Perhaps I still don't see it," Davis offered from the
window. He hadn't really seemed to be listening at all.

It was Captain Maury who spoke next, and though
his words sounded as if he were talking down to the
President, his voice was as gentle as if he were explaining something unpleasant to a little child. "Well,
just incidentally to the main operation so far, thanks
to the lieutenant here, we are going to shut down one
Railroad station close to Richmond, which has undoubtedly been bleeding away men and secrets for
years. But think, if one of our agents, pretending to be
working for Lafayette Baker, could traverse the whole
line from here to Georgia or even farther, we could roll
the whole thing up. Put the traitors out of communication with each other, perhaps permanently. Catch
thousands more of those hundred thousand deserters
who could win the war for us in an afternoon if they'd
just do their duty. Hang a Yankee spy from every
bridge between here and Montgomery. Just to replace
their lost men would take Baker and Pinkerton a couple of years at a minimum, and during that time their

best new recruits would all be headed south, not hunting our men in the North, so that we might stand a much better chance of penetrating their secrets."

Davis nodded slowly. "It isn't going to result in more shooting in Richmond, is it? Gentlemen, I know that my concern is selfish, but Varina has not slept well—"

"Mr. President, I think if we manage this properly, there will be no more shooting—at least not from this cause—in Richmond." Kindly, as if assisting a very old man, Captain Maury assisted Jefferson Davis to his feet and guided him out. While they waited, General Alexander and Dan Samson eyed each other, but found nothing much to say.

When Maury returned, his usually lively face was drawn and sad. "I hate to see that," he said. "I simply hate to see it."

Samson must have looked puzzled, because the captain turned to him and said, "Of course, you've been out of touch with the news, so you wouldn't know. Little Joe Davis—the poor child was only five— fell off a balcony and was killed a week ago today. The mother is still in bed with shock, and I can't imagine what it must be like at nighttime for the President. Thank God we've got Pickett and Beauregard and Lee to keep the Yankees out, because just now I don't think the President could muster the interest if they were banging on his door."

Alexander rose. "Well, the business seems clear enough. There is one detail, however, that both you and the President are forgetting, Maury, and we certainly need to inform Lieutenant Heller of. Of that whole list of prisoners he was to free for Lafayette Baker, the only one still alive and in Castle Thunder is Telemachus Carelias, and he's not in much shape to travel. We can only hope the Carelias girl will feel enough loyalty to her father, since she doesn't to her country, to want him to escape anyway, and that this nigger-spy of Baker's will not decide to just give up the whole thing. But then, if they do abandon it, Heller can no doubt just arrest them and we'll be no worse off than before. Come around to my building in half an hour, Lieutenant, and I'll have the appropriate papers waiting for you."

"Thank you, sir."

He was gone quickly, seeing himself out. Captain Maury paused a moment and then smiled. "Well, well, you can see that you've caused us all some trouble, but then I suppose that's to be expected. Go downstairs and have lunch with Reynolds before you go to pick up your papers—that's an order. It means so much to him when one of 'his boys' comes back."

As Samson left, he saw that Maury was already bending over a lump of rock, probably one of the many brought up during the laying of the transatlantic cable, magnifying glass in one hand, pen in the other, a sandwich unattended on the desk. As he went back down the stairs to his lunch with Reynolds, he wondered what kind of world would take a kind, intelligent man like Maury, who wanted nothing more than to know a little more of nature's secrets, and put him in charge of sending mixed-up kids like Prescott Heller to their deaths.

Not a world as I would have made it, either, Master Xi whispered, *but then it was never up to either of us, Daniel Samson.*

GENERAL ALEXANDER WAS certainly efficient. He had already arranged the necessary papers so that Prescott Heller, in his already created identity as Sean Toole, County Limerick, Ireland, U.K., would be allowed to take out Telemachus Carelias, now supposed to be a distant cousin, on a flag-of-truce ship to Ireland, where he was to be treated for "disorders acquired while in prison." After all the elaborate troubles thus far, Samson would be able to just walk into Castle Thunder and walk out with Caroline's father. Something about that seemed grossly unfair.

Along with the orders was a short personal note from General Alexander.

Every so often Maury trusts too much to the ingenuity of subordinates. You will need to communicate often with these offices during your journey south. I have taken the liberty to make you an appointment with one of our most trusted agents, at the Broad Street Theater, for two o'clock this afternoon. This should leave you plenty of time to reach your scheduled rendezvous with the two federal agents. My man will inform you extensively of the locations and names of our agents likely to be found along your route, so that you can use them as mail drops as you go and so that you need never be far from friends.

It was a thoughtful thing to include, Samson realized, even if it added a little complexity to the afternoon. And certainly acquiring the names and addresses of twenty or fifty Confederate counter Intelligence agents had to be useful to him, and possibly useful to Baker, assuming that "Sean Toole" ever returned to federal lines alive.

He wondered how Caroline and Juky were doing. He hoped they were able to get at least food and rest, and a little time in some fairly safe spot. He felt almost guilty for being able to just stroll up Ninth Street, past the Capitol, toward Broad, without having to fear anything.

The statue of George Washington stood as it always had, facing south so that the horse's rump, as had often been pointed out, was turned toward the city of Washington. The Capitol itself was undisturbed by the war, thus far. If an observer looked just a bit above human head level, so that the gray uniforms didn't cross the path of his eyes, he could easily imagine that this was any peaceful day in 1840, or 1990, for that matter.

The streets were still full of people on various business, even if inflation was roaring, and many shop windows were empty, and there was getting to be a hungry, dilapidated look about the town. Richmond was obviously a capital at war, but not yet one that felt itself to be losing.

He had almost reached Broad Street, having just passed the corner of Ninth and Grace, when he heard the high whistles from Broad Street, the universal signal among the street vendors and beggars that meant the dogcatchers were on the move up there. Without hurrying or hesitating, seemingly as if he had only forgotten some annoying small thing at home, Samson turned and headed up Grace Street.

As soon as he was away from the Capitol, the foot traffic thinned out and he was able to walk much faster. True, he had papers that could get him released from the automatic draft that applied to every male in the streets who looked anything vaguely between eighteen and thirty-five years old, but to get released he would first have to be presented to the commander of the watch, and that would take hours or even days that he didn't have. It was a minor annoyance, familiar to any Confederate officer on leave who had ever gone out in his civilian clothes. There were stories of full colonels on three-day furloughs, swept up by the dogcatchers on the first day of the furlough after breakfast and in deep trouble with their CO when they finally were able to get released and get back to their units again, sometimes a full week later. Most of the time, however, the population was alert enough so that the dogcatchers caught no one.

Chances were they would make a sweep of Broad Street, where the crowds were thick. By the time they had worked their way up to Broad and Seventh, where the theater was, Samson would already be safely inside, but just to take no chances, he would go in on the Seventh Street side.

He passed the tall spire of the Catholic church. Two blocks to go. He no longer heard the whistles . . . until he heard them behind him. Just his luck that there was some zealot in charge who was sweeping the back streets for a change.

Samson darted right around the Catholic church and headed up Eighth, hoping that he wasn't really getting himself trapped between two parties of dog-catchers. But he was. He angled into an alley that almost certainly would come out on the back side of the Broad Street Theater, and now that he was out of their sight, he launched into a serious dead run.

Behind him he could hear the shouting. It sounded as though they had grabbed four or five men. Hooves clattered on the bricks of the alley behind him as Samson reached its end.

Naturally enough, early in the afternoon, the back doors of the Broad Street Theater were bolted.

He zigged left, around the side of the building from whence he could hear a tinny piano repeating scales over and over as several voices sang "la-la-la" patterns after them. Sure enough, he could hear because there was an open window, its lower sill just about the height of the top of his head.

With no hesitation, he leaped up, grabbed the sill, chinned himself in through the window and jumped inside. There were half a dozen shrieks as young ladies scattered in different directions, probably assuming he was a crazed stage-door johnnie. He found himself backstage, heavy curtains hanging all around, facing a squat, muscular man who was seated at the piano. The man had quietly pulled a pistol from somewhere and had it leveled on Samson's chest.

Samson slowly raised his hands and took two steps back to get himself out of the line of sight of the window. The dogcatchers were subject to a "hot pursuit" rule—unless someone fleeing them was actually seen in a building or running into it, they couldn't enter the building. So he was safe enough now, assuming none of the chorus girls ran out into the street to turn him in.

"I really hope," he said, "that the phrase 'there are two roses on every path' means something to you."

"The phrase means nothing," the man said, "but give the countersign anyway, if you know it."

"I have no idea what it is."

Pocketing the pistol, the pianist grinned at him. "That's easily the silliest set of countersigns Alexander's office has come up with yet. All right, young man, what can I do for you?"

Samson presented the note from General Alexander, and the burly man nodded. "Yes, I can tell you most of what you need to know, and what I can't tell you, you can probably improvise. I do hope you've got a good memory, because this material really must not be committed to paper under any circumstances."

The way the man spoke had an odd, rolling quality to it. It took Samson a moment's search in Prescott Heller's memories to realize that it was the kind of voice that Heller would have identified with the stage. Indeed, Heller had seen this man act at one time or another, though the name was eluding him.

Samson turned his full attention to learning the directions for finding each War Department Secret Service agent along the line of the Appalachians—which both he and the actor agreed was the most probable way the Railroad would turn out to run—and more importantly, the signs and signals used in each part of the route.

The actor was friendly and courteous, but he was also an iron taskmaster. In two hours, Samson had the list down cold, along with a minor headache. At last the actor pronounced him satisfactory on the whole business. "That should get you through the South," he said, "as long as the Railroad obligingly runs close to our agents. Which, of course, it won't do. Improvisation's the soul of art, boy, make sure you can improvise when it's needed, because this is no game for anyone who just stays on the script." He clapped him on his shoulder in a friendly way, and the dark eyes seemed to burn deep into Samson's. "Now good luck, and keep your wits about you. Once we get this war won, we're going to need intelligent young men."

Samson was walking up the aisle, and the actor was seated at the piano down in front of the stage, playing something softly, when the name that Heller had been unable to think of matched up with a name that was in Samson's memory—a name that would have been in almost any American's memory.

Without a moment's thought, Samson turned in the dark of the aisle, drew his Colt revolver, looked at the wide, strong back bent over the piano, cocked the hammer, sighted carefully, squeezed the trigger—

Somehow the mechanism froze, and he felt Heller regain, for just an instant, control of the body, and nothing at all happened. He uncocked it, returned it to his belt and left the building. Inside his head, although he now had physical control back, he could hear the wild, nasty, shouting laughter of Prescott Heller, and the actor's name, over and over.

John Wilkes Booth.

Samson remembered that it was still a hot controversy at home about whether or not he had been a Confederate agent. Well, now he knew, but who could he tell? He would try to drop a message through the Railroad, but—

Whoever you entrusted that message to would lose it or would be killed, Master Xi said in his mind. *And if Heller had not been there to seize control of your trigger finger, just as easily the gun would have misfired, the cartridge would have proven a dud, you would have missed...you are not back here to change the past! You cannot alter what has happened, but only the role you had in it!*

I know, I know, I know, Samson thought. I know that, but...he raked through Heller's mind and found that meeting with Lincoln again, the tall man's warm brown eyes looking into him, accepting him as he was, the face that every American knew by heart, looking into his own.

But I had to try, Master Xi. I had to try.

Even Heller seemed to understand, for he became quiet, and as Daniel Samson walked quickly and quietly through the crowded afternoon streets of Richmond, his thoughts were all but empty of anything other than the tiny chapel where he was to meet Juky and Caroline. Suddenly, despite the teenage body he had in this time, he felt centuries old.

6

The little Methodist chapel was on a quiet side street, not far from Jefferson Davis's house. It was ideal because there was an African church around the corner from it. Both were places where people often went to sit and quietly pray, so that just hanging around until the rest of the group showed would be uncomplicated. Samson had gotten there first and was sitting in one of the side pews where he could watch the door out of the corner of his eye. It was roasting hot, as spring in Virginia often was, and heat beat in through the door in an almost painful way.

The woman who entered didn't look anything like Caroline until she sat down next to him. Her hair was now a deep, rich brown, and she wore it differently, along with a pair of glasses that were probably plain glass. Also, it looked as if she had acquired a different corset, though Samson would have bet plenty that she still had the dueling pistols handy.

"Edwin," she said without preface, "we thought we might find you here. There's been terrible trouble at home. Jupiter's brought the trap. Please come at once."

Samson followed her out the door, and there was Juky, dressed in full coachman's regalia, seated on the little carriage. All right, his name was now Edwin, and Juky was clearly Jupiter. He just hoped Caroline would find a way to tell him what name she was going under.

"Where to, Miz Mary Ann?" Juky asked, and that completed the picture as far as was needed. They wove through side streets, taking their time, not speaking, working their way north. Samson wasn't sure where they were going, but he figured that if Caroline had found a way to be provided with clothing and supplies on this order, it was somewhere friendly.

The little house was on Charity Street, up in the northernmost part of the city. It was a plain wood-frame place, a little cleaner and better maintained than other houses in the neighborhood, but not otherwise much different from them. When the trap rolled to a stop in front of the house, Samson got down and assisted Caroline, and Juky drove on, obviously circling around to bring the trap in through the alley to the back of the house.

He still suspected nothing until the very moment that the rope dropped around his shoulders and strong hands pinned his arms back. He stifled the urge to cry out, wanting to spin and see if he could kick whoever would be grabbing Caroline, give her a chance to get away, but his feet were swept from under him, and he saw her walk unconcernedly by as four big men pinned him down and tied him.

In a minute they had carried him into the shuttered and darkened back parlor of the house, and he found himself seated on a small chair in front of a long, narrow table. At the table sat three men, one clearly wearing a Confederate officer's uniform, and all wearing dark, heavy hoods of burlap painted black. Two candles burned in front of him, and they were the only light the room had. The black shadows of the hooded men fell onto the wall behind them, darkening the Stars and Stripes pinned to the back wall.

"State your name," the central figure said.

"Sean Toole. First lieutenant. First District of Columbia Cavalry." He was trying to remember if there was any equivalent to a serial number, and trying more frantically to figure out which side had him and for what.

"Are you sure it isn't Prescott Heller, first lieutenant, detached service to the Submarine Battery Service?" Juky's voice said behind him. He had never heard so much ice in a human voice before.

"I have operated under that name, as well," he said quietly.

"But there *is* a Heller family, they *do* have a son named Prescott and he *was* a cadet at the Virginia Military Institute," the figure in the Confederate uniform said softly.

Samson's blood froze to rasping, painful slush in every one of his veins. Now he knew—the Peace Society, or one of the other anti-Confederate resistance organizations. And they knew all about Prescott Heller being a double agent.

He wondered how many formalities they would go through before they killed him and whether he would be tortured for information first.

He wondered whether Juky had suspected him and had him investigated, or if perhaps the idea had come as an unpleasant shock to his comrade.

He wondered what Caroline thought.

The main judge was speaking. "Call the first witness."

It was Caroline. She didn't look at him, and her voice was so soft that several times the judge had to ask her to repeat herself. Her hands knotted, clenched and wrung each other in her lap as she spoke, but she made herself go on.

She told the story from the beginning: the mission, the bad luck that seemed to dog it, Samson's success in overpowering the guards at the last minute, Jim Strang's death... By the end of it, Samson would have voted to convict himself. She was clearly trying hard to be fair, not giving him any breaks but not loading it against him, either, just letting the facts do the talking. The trouble was that the facts said he was ripe for a noose.

When Juky testified, it was no better for Samson. There were things Juky, as an experienced agent, had noticed, and some of them were in Samson's favor. For one thing, the operation itself was too small and unimportant for Samson to have been authorized to kill Confederate soldiers as he had done. On the other hand, it turned out that Juky had also observed some small but significant pauses and lapses of mind that were most easily explained by Samson's maintaining a cover. So although Juky confused the case with his careful, dry testimony, it didn't look any better for Samson when he was done.

The center judged asked, "Juky, all of us here respect your opinion. What do you think is really going on with Lieutenant Heller here?"

Juky pulled one earlobe thoughtfully. "I truly can't say myself, sir. He's acted so thoroughly like one of us and yet so completely like one of them, my only guess would be that he may be some kind of a rogue agent, doing all of this for himself, perhaps hoping to have a hostage who would be of value to both sides and to get them bidding against each other."

"Or perhaps working for the British or French," the judge in the Confederate uniform suggested. "We know Britain has been supplying covert aid to both sides, in the hope of favors no matter who wins. And the French have done everything in their power to keep the war going so that neither the Union nor the Confederate side would be in a position to put a stop to their meddling in Mexico. So he might also be playing both sides against the middle for them."

The candles flickered and danced in a stray breeze, and the dark, hooded shadows swayed back and forth ominously across the Stars and Stripes. Samson had the sudden, absurd thought of telling them what was really going on, and calling Master Xi to testify. The problem here was that he needed to make up something that was a lot more convincing than the truth.

The ropes bit into his wrists. They had known what they were doing when they tied him up, right down to the little trick of tying his feet to the chair legs so that, even if he were to shake off a binding, he could go nowhere fast. It wasn't even worth squirming.

There were two more witnesses. One, he suspected, was a cadet from VMI, since he was quite young, and identified Dan as Prescott Heller but said little else. The other described shadowing Samson to the Submarine Battery Service building, seeing Jefferson Davis and General Alexander leaving and seeing Samson visit Alexander's office. That one was probably a cab driver, Samson thought, or possibly one of the flower sellers or newspaper vendors who had been on the sidewalk that morning, or just possibly a detective in the Maury or Alexander organizations who had turned his coat quietly.

What was he going to say? Assuming, of course, that they allowed him to say anything in his own defense, and didn't just execute him.

"If the prisoner would care to offer an explanation or to ask any questions," the center judge said, "this court will now listen and respond."

"I assume I'm facing the death penalty," Samson said. "I don't imagine there's much else you're in a position to inflict."

"That's correct."

Well, here it was, then. As much of the truth as he could manage would have to do.

"It is true that I was recruited in the summer of 1861 by Captain Maury, during my freshman year at VMI, and served the CSA faithfully as a secret agent until the summer of 1863. Then I was sent north to join Baker's secret service and thus provide a spy within that service for the Confederacy. The reason you find my behavior inconsistent since that time is that I have gradually become pro-Union, but I confess I felt myself very much bound by my previous oath of service. So I did not reveal myself to Lafayette Baker, which is what I should have done, nor did I stop sending reports to the Confederacy, since I thought my position as agent there might be useful.

"I had not realized that they would be able to deduce everything about our mission from the reports I sent them, but that is what they did. In that regard, I was foolish.

"At any rate, I've fought and shed blood on the Union side now, and it is to that side I belong, whether you believe me or not, even if I am hanged as an agent of the other side. I've done a lot of things that are really foolish, and if you want to hang me I can't say I blame you, but that's the truth."

Smugly the Prescott Heller part of his mind pointed out that he sounded like a real idiot.

"What did you talk to Captain Maury about?" the central judge asked.

Samson held nothing back and told him the whole conversation. "So the upshot of it is that I have a pass that will get me into Castle Thunder and get me out with Telemachus Carelias. Apparently several of the men we were sent to rescue have been moved to other prisons or executed. He's the only one on the list still there.''

''We've confirmed that much, at least,'' said the uniformed judge.

The judge in the center drummed his fingers on the table. ''This is not going to be an easy decision. I'd like to ask my fellow jurists to step into the next room with me for a moment.''

When the door closed behind them, there was no sound in the room except for breathing. The two witnesses that Samson didn't know seemed to be quite uncomfortable. Samson twisted around to see what everyone was doing. Juky was sitting quietly by one of the heavily curtained windows, apparently staring at nothing a few feet in front of him. Caroline sat in the corner, head bowed, looking no happier.

In the next room, voices were not raised, but there was considerable excitement in the low buzz. Obviously they were having a hard time deciding what to do. After a long period of time during which Samson felt sweat running down his face into his eyes, he felt a touch on his forehead and looked up to see Caroline quietly wiping his brow with her handkerchief.

He whispered, ''Thanks.'' She nodded just slightly, but whether she was helping him out of affection or just because she wasn't the type to let anyone just sit and suffer, he had no idea.

After she sat back down, she seemed to fidget more than before, but then again it was quite possible that her new clothes weren't quite a perfect fit.

At last the judges came back in. "Before we pronounce a verdict," the head judge said, "recite the information that Booth gave you at the theater."

Prescott Heller grieved in the back of his mind as he did it, but Samson recited slowly and carefully, making sure he got all of it right as the judges took their notes. As he finished, the head judge nodded. "The information is accurate on four of the agents, to my knowledge."

"Three, to mine," said the uniformed one.

"Six." The last of the judges seemed to waver, as if he had something else to say.

"Then we are agreed?" the head judge said.

"We are," the other two said in unison. In a few minutes they had untied Samson.

"Let us make it clear to you what we are—and are not—doing. We cannot make a decision to convict or acquit based on what we know thus far. A transcription of all of this is being forwarded to Baker's office, including the very important information that Booth is a spy, though we've all suspected that for a long time. He's due for a tour of the Northern states next year, and if Baker knows, he should be able to use him to feed false information to the Confederacy and to neutralize any harm he might do."

"He's extremely dangerous," Samson said, and felt his throat constricting. He knew he would be unable to say more if he tried.

"We'll note that, of course. At any rate, if and when you return to federal lines, you will become Baker's problem. Meanwhile, we intend to have the use of your pass into Castle Thunder. You are paroled from us on the condition that you go at once to Castle Thunder, get Telemachus Carelias and bring him out. You will do this with Juky and with Miss Carelias so that it looks as if your original plan were being followed. You will then drive across the Mayo Bridge into Manchester and make a right turn onto Harrison Street, and drive slowly up that street, as if searching for an address.

"At some point you will be set upon by armed men. Mr. and Miss Carelias and Juky will be apparently carried off, and will really be taken in by our organization and taken to safe places where they can be effective. You may receive a few harmless blows and be knocked down into the mud, but you will be otherwise unhurt. What happens after that is quite up to you. You can either go back to the federal lines, getting there by whatever means you can manage, and see if you can convince Lafayette Baker and thus escape a hanging over there, or if your true masters are on this side of the line, you can go to them. With, naturally, the understanding that if we ever catch you again, you will be a dead man." The figure faced him in a completely relaxed position, like some of the martial-arts masters Samson had known. "Will you accept?"

"I wasn't aware I had a choice."

"You could choose to be executed, or try to escape from us here. By all accounts you are preternaturally skilled at bare-handed fighting."

"I'll take my chances on completing the original mission," Samson said. "How soon do we leave?"

"It better be soon," Juky said softly from the window. "Same man's gone by this side of the building four times in twenty minutes. I got a feeling we were followed. Sorry about that—I thought we had lost them."

"It happens," the head judge said. "Do you think there are armed men anywhere in quantity?"

"If there were, and they knew who was in here, they'd have rushed the house," Juky said. "Probably one man who's sent for help. Getting dark out there... bet he's nervous."

"He should be," said the uniformed judge. "Lieutenant Heller is going to kill him."

That seemed to take everyone in the room aback, and even the candle guttered wildly, but Samson saw the sense in it at once; it was an early loyalty test before they committed valuable agents to an extremely dangerous situation.

"Bare steel, I assume," Samson said. "You don't want the sound of a shot. And you don't want him to cry out."

They all nodded. By now the other judges had seen the uniformed one's point.

Quick and soft as a shadow, Samson was out the window. Years of experience and practice at *ninjutsu* took over. There was an enemy to be disposed of, and so his mind locked down on the single task.

He had emerged from a window that was shrouded by the deep shadow of late evening—the sun had al-

most set—and crept along a hedge, timing it so that
the "aimlessly" wandering watcher was on the other
side of the house. Samson crouched in a deep shadow
and watched him from underneath a bush.

The back of his neck prickled, and he almost looked
behind him before he realized what had been giving
him such intense suspicion. This lone man wandering
on this dusty moonlit sidestreet was not only watching the house from which Samson had emerged. He
was also taking a quick glance at the end of each trip
up and down the block, a glance toward something
near the house rather than the house itself, and something about the awkwardness and the tension of that
glance told Samson a great deal.

These had to be Alexander's men, because they were
working in pairs. Alexander hated to lose an agent,
and so insisted on more safety measures than either
Baker or Maury commonly did. As Samson's eyes
adjusted to the dim, he eventually picked out the
sniper sitting in the tree. Luckily the sniper was on this
side of the street. The man in the street was doing the
bulk of the watching, but the sniper could see the back
alley if need be, and provided cover for the man
walking up and down the middle of the street, so that
if anything were attempted on him, the ambush could
be ambushed.

Samson shrugged. Good tactics, but since the
backup hadn't gotten here yet, not good enough. He
wriggled forward on his belly and waited for the moment when the man walking the street would be concentrating on trying to get glimpses through the cracks

in the curtains. What would he see? Mostly eyeballs staring out, Samson suspected.

As the moment came, Samson raced forward, soundlessly leaped upward, swung up into the branches and crept toward the sniper.

Fortunately the sniper had stayed low in the tree, and the limb he was on was as stable as the ground. The sniper was stretched out on it, lying prone with his rifle stock under him in the basic prone firing position.

If that rifle fell into the street, everything would get much more complicated. And Samson didn't see much way to prevent it, other than plain old dumb luck.

Well, then, he would just have to be lucky, so it would just have to be complicated. He edged forward along the branch, bowie knife drawn, and at last dropped on top of his opponent. As the sniper reared back to shout, Samson's left arm snaked around his throat and grabbed far up the collar on the other side, pulling tight at once with the hard, bony edge of Samson's hand closing off the windpipe. Not as neat as pinching the carotid, but it would have to do.

The bowie knife slipped in under the ribs on the man's back cleanly and neatly, puncturing each kidney, two hard, fast strokes that meant the man was already dying. Then as he arched his back in agony, Samson slid the knife down deep between the man's thighs and severed the left femoral artery, bringing another gush of blood and effectively dropping the man's blood pressure, between the three huge holes just opened in his circulatory system, to zero.

Thus he was probably already unconscious from shock as Samson turned the knife against the thighbone in a quick, scraping twist and slashed across to get the right femoral artery, as well, incidentally removing the man's genitalia. Finally Samson lifted the dying man's head with the edge of his arm and slashed his carotid and windpipe so deeply that he felt the tip of the bowie knife nick the spine.

It had taken him about four seconds in total to administer the Five Cut Death, and now he lay on top of the oozing corpse, his feet and one hand stabilizing him on the rough bark of the tree as the man walking the street turned, looked, saw in the rapidly fading light only that there was still something in the tree and he was still visible to it, and came back the other way.

It was about ten feet to the ground, Samson reckoned. At least he had a hell of a good diversion here, but he was going to have to be very careful about possibly turning an ankle, and he would certainly need another change of clothing, judging by the warm, wet feeling he had all over the front of his shirt and pants. Mercifully the rifle had stayed pinned in the crook of the tree by the body's weight.

As the watcher in the street passed below, carefully not looking up so as not to give away the sniper's position, Samson rolled the leaking body out from under him and let it drop directly in front of the enemy. It hit in an untidy windmill of flailing arms and legs, like a rag doll, and lay on its back, the huge second mouth Samson had opened in the throat pulled wide open in a ghastly red grin. The walking man froze in horror, and that was the last thing he ever did consciously. Samson dropped straight onto him, seizing his neck and turning his head sideways under Samson's arm, then flipping forward in the hard somersault that follows the line of the soft, nonvital parts of the body. That, and the absorption of force by his victim, had Samson leaping to his feet with no more than a little twinge of pain where the fleshy part of his shoulder had rolled a little hard going down. But it whipped the Confederate agent around hard by his already bent neck, and with a crunch of bone and cartilage, the man's spine was wrenched apart just above the base of his neck. He was certainly unable to make any noise and would be dead in a minute or less anyway, but Samson administered the coup de grace in one quick slash across the carotid anyway. He didn't want to think of the man lying there paralyzed, feeling life ebb away, perhaps feeling pain but being unable to do anything about it.

He stood up, glanced cautiously around and waved the all-clear to the people inside the house. An instant later the men, still hooded, emerged with Juky, carrying one of the carpets rolled up, and the two bodies were moved onto it and carried carefully into the building.

"We'll have to burn this place anyway. If they got a message off, it's no longer safe," the quiet judge said.

The chief nodded. "We'll put the bodies in the middle of the room and douse them with lamp oil. Throw a little on the curtains, as well, and this old termite palace will go up like a match head." He turned to Samson. "You've convinced me, anyway. I certainly wouldn't believe that Maury, let alone Alexander, would send two men to be killed just so you could convince us. We had a change of clothes ready for you in case of acquittal. You'd best just step into a tub of water here, wash up quickly and get out of that bloody mess you're wearing. In case they're recognizable, we'll need to leave the clothes you have on on top of the bodies so that they burn, too."

Samson nodded and stripped, no longer caring about whatever standard of modesty might be applicable at this time and place. Besides, the only woman present knew perfectly well what he was like naked. He stepped into the washtub and, using a couple of rags, managed to get the worst of the gore off himself. He used a couple more to get sort of dry before getting into his "new" clothing. He noted with some amusement that Caroline had obviously remembered his sizes exactly.

As he shrugged on his coat, the chief judge said, "Well, I trust you enough to unhood. And if you're not really native to Richmond, you won't know me anyway." He revealed a square bull neck, an almost completely bald head and a heavy mustache and sideburns. There was something overwhelmingly familiar about him. "That was pretty fancy knife work. Which side did you learn that on? They sure don't teach that to the cadets at VMI."

Samson shrugged. "I studied with some experts on my own. Seemed like something I would want to know."

By now they had piled his bloody old clothes on top of the two corpses rolled in the shabby old rug. Juky made sure the fireplace damper was open wide for a strong draft, and then poured the lamp oil, dashing the last of it onto the curtains. "Time we rolled, sirs."

"Time indeed," the chief agreed. They were out the door in moments. The chief turned to strike a match, threw it into his box of matches and tossed the blazing box onto the rolled rug, which went up with a roar. "Hope the city fire brigade can manage this, short-handed as they are, but I hope they don't manage it too quickly. Be a good thing if they couldn't tell how their men died, or even if those were their men. All right, Heller, you've half proved yourself. Go get Telemachus out of the pen, follow orders afterward, get back to Washington alive and maybe Cousin Lafayette will hear something to your credit. You might not even do time in prison."

As Samson rode between Caroline and Juky in the trap, his mind clicked. *Cousin Lafayette.* Well, that explained why the man had seemed so familiar—just one more Baker cousin out of God knew how many working for the Secret Service. Heller had met four of them and had heard of more.

Beside him, Caroline quietly said, "Are you telling the truth now?"

"I'm on the side I say I'm on, and I'll do my best to carry out the mission we're on," he said, not wanting to lie to her even slightly.

"So you have more secrets?" She seemed to sit back from him.

"Nothing that would cause you pain if I were free to tell you."

There was a very long pause, and then Juky spoke, his voice so soft that it barely carried over the creaking of the wagon. "Miss Carelias, I've never seen two young people want each other worse. And it sounds to me like he's trying real hard to tell you the truth without breaking any promises he ought to keep. That bespeaks honor more than it does ill intentions. I think you ought to tell him—there's a good chance one of you could be dead tonight, and it wouldn't be good if it went unsaid."

"Tell him what?" Caroline asked.

"What's in your heart."

She sighed. "What's in it right now is all fear and confusion. And I was so happy this morning despite the danger. Now that I know what can happen..." She leaned against Samson and breathed in his ear. "Oh, Daniel, damn it, will you at least tell me you learned to butcher men with a knife so quickly and thoroughly for some decent reason, that it's not because you like it? Because no matter what else, I don't want to think of giving myself to a man who's just a thug and a beast underneath."

"I didn't learn how to do that because I like it. It was something I had to know how to do once, as part of my duty, so I learned," Samson muttered, looking down at the floorboards. "And I don't think I'm going to live much longer, so I think I'll just tell you that I love you, that I feel like I've always loved you, that no matter what, I'll find a way to see you again, this side or the other of the grave." He felt Master Xi reach to choke him from saying too much, then relax as he realized that Samson would stay within the bounds.

What she whispered to him then he would treasure through more than a thousand lifetimes to come. He would hear it again from her lips in other centuries, other places, other languages, but it would never be sweeter than it was now.

When he glanced up, Juky appeared to have taken up astronomy, for he was studying the night sky with remarkable care.

CASTLE THUNDER WAS an imposing place even in the daytime, and at night with the extra gaslights illuminating the area around it, it was one of the more striking places in Richmond. It was four stories high, counting its attic rooms, with heavy bars set over the first-floor windows. The wide doors where tobacco wagons had once rolled into it were mostly bricked up now, leaving only a narrow entryway guarded by two sentinels. In shape it was long and narrow, so that it looked taller than it actually was, but still it was a good fifteen-foot drop from the second-floor windows to the ground, enough to deter most men even without the bars and the guards. The "dead line"—a line of narrow wooden boards nailed to stakes, called that because if a prisoner touched or crossed it without permission, the guards were under orders to shoot to kill—was a scant few feet from the front of the building.

It was really just an effect caused by the fact that it was a dark redbrick building that had stood for a long time in a city that burned soft coal, but the building had a dark color in the flickering gas lamps as if it were made of freshly congealed blood. On the other hand, the smell of death and sewage that clung to Castle Thunder in the warm spring air was no accident.

Rather than leave Juky with the carriage, they took him in with them. If trouble started, there would be nothing he could do out there, but an extra gun, or knife or set of fists might make all the difference inside. The letter Samson carried got them past the sentinels with no trouble at all. Clearly the orders had been given, though it might be only orders for a trap.

The officer of the watch was a grizzled old fellow wearing an odd decoration on his gray uniform. Looking closely, Samson realized it was a campaign medal from the War of 1812. This was obviously a member of the Invalid Corps, the men who were unable to serve in the combat arm for some physical reason but had volunteered to join the Army and were used to free able-bodied men to fight.

He nodded over the papers, then turned to Caroline and said, "Miss Carelias, I feel must tell you. We have tried to maintain a decent prison here, but we haven't always succeeded. Food and sanitation have not been what they should, and for a man of your father's years, that has taken a great toll. And, of course, because we've held so many deserters and traitors here, we've had a very high percentage of prisoners executed.... Which means, of course, that a generous man like your father was constantly looking after younger men who were frightened or had to settle their affairs. Well, on my own and I would swear to whatever gods that I had *not* said this if ever you quote me, Miss Carelias . . . your father has worked so hard to keep up the spirits of so many men who have perished on the gallows or the dead line, that it has finally left him a broken man. He is not the man who came in here two years ago, and there's no denying it.''

The old man sighed unhappily. ''I tell you this because when you see him, it is going to be a shock, but if you are prepared, he need not see that shock in your face. We can at least spare him that much. And Mr. Toole, I must say your coming is a blessing. To be somewhere far away from his torn and bleeding country is just what Mr. Carelias needs.''

He went off down the hallway, leaving them in the office. It was not a safe place to speak, but Samson reached out and squeezed Caroline's hand. She returned the pressure with a grip that was suddenly like that of a vise.

It was several long breaths before she let go of his hand.

They heard the clanking of the leg irons a long time before Telemachus Carelias was brought to them. Outside the door to the office, a few feet from where they listened, they heard one of the big, brawny guards wielding the chisel to cut through the iron rivets that held the leg irons together.

Something about the sound made it the most unnerving thing Samson had ever heard. But as he looked around he saw that the effect was worse on Caroline, imagining her father having endured them for so long, and worst of all on Juky, who had heard that sound far too many times in his life.

Even Prescott Heller seemed disgusted by it.

When they brought him in, Samson recognized him from Caroline's description—the wide white sideburns, bedraggled looking now, myopic squint, sharp little nose and the red, fleshy face were as he had expected.

But in another sense nothing was as expected. The man was like a ruined house that people had fled from long ago, leaving the house still making noises only because of squirrels in the attic, rats in the basement, and the slow settling of the foundation. Every few seconds a violent nervous twitch would run across Telemachus Carelias's left cheek. He had a shuffling walk that was only partly from the leg irons and had much more to do with not quite trusting himself to walk. As he came in, he first stared vacantly into space for a long moment, then turned slowly toward Caroline like an electronic toy whose batteries were almost gone.

Then he saw Caroline, and a grin split his face and for one moment light came back into his eyes. She ran to him and held him, and his arms went around her. But even as Samson watched, the alertness left his eyes, and the arms around Caroline grew slack. When she pulled back to look at him, there were tears running out of his pale blue eyes, and his lips were moving irregularly.

"What is it, Father?"

"I can't remember." He shook his head slowly. "I can't remember anything at all....Things get lost. How's your mother?"

She had been dead for six years.

Caroline turned toward the old officer of the watch. He refused to let her catch his eye, and Samson realized how embarrassed the man was by the situation.

Prisons were never easy places to run decently, the Confederacy was broke anyway, and there had been very little the jailers here could do. An officer could make things much worse—people like Wirz at Andersonville certainly were—but he couldn't make things any better. And aside from that, there was the simple reality that a dark, almost airless, foul-smelling prison was no place for an old man who had never known anything but comfort and gentility all his life.

Telemachus Carelias was a wreck of a man, and nothing and no one could restore him now. No wonder Alexander and Maury had been perfectly willing to see him go free.

There was nothing to be done. Samson gave the embarrassed old officer a brief nod in thanks for his courtesy, and they put a couple of shawls around old Carelias and took him out, showing their pass to the sentinels. In a few minutes they were headed down Cary Street toward the Mayo Bridge, the same bridge they had crossed only twenty-four hours before.

Caroline didn't speak as they drove, but her father did. It was the prattle of a child: what had been served for breakfast—boiled corn with a little bacon, about a cup of it—the names of the people living in the room he shared with them, the sorts of things that a little kid would tell you about staying in the hospital to have his tonsils out. Every so often he would start to tell a story and begin to weep when he lost his place, but after a few long harsh sobs he would stop, stare slackly for a few long breaths and then begin again. Every so often he would ask Caroline who these people were and if they were going to another prison.

The next time he said anything coherent, it was "My daughter, that's Caroline, that Caroline, she doesn't like me, damned if she does, she's sitting there making faces at her old father, I ought to spank the young scamp, I should, not liking her father, she's making faces at me." He began to weep heavily without stopping.

Juky touched Samson, next to him on the driver's seat, with a light elbow, and jerked his head toward the back. Samson swallowed hard, but Juky was right, so he climbed back over the seat.

Caroline was sitting stock-still, staring down at the floor, silent tears moving erratically down her cheeks. Gently Samson put an arm around her.

She leaned against him just a little, but otherwise she said nothing.

The iron rims of the wheels of the little trap made a grinding thunder on the planking of the bridge, empty now after sunset because of the military curfew. Sam-

son just hoped no patrols would question their papers
because even though they were really in order, a delay
right now could be as fatal as an arrest. But the sentries at the Richmond end of the bridge didn't seem to
have any problem with them, nor did the sentries at
the Manchester end.

They were on Hull Street, and the dark houses of
Manchester rolled by. In wartime, with fuel short, the
city went to bed early, and out here in the residential
areas few if any lights were on. Half a dozen blocks at
most, and Samson would have to leave the trap. He
needed to say so much to Caroline, to comfort her, to
let her know how worried he was about her, to say how
sorry he was that things had turned out like this, but
he seemed to have no voice and no words.

The turn onto Harrison Street came, and he let his
arm close a little tighter around her and squeezed her
shoulder. "Almost time," he said, feeling like a fool.

"Stay alive. You find me, or I'll find you," she
whispered back.

"I will."

There was a lurch as Juky brought the little trap to
a quick stop, and when Samson looked up there were
horsemen around them, all of them hooded. One of
them gestured with an old flintlock rifle, and Samson
got out of the carriage with a last squeeze of hands
with Caroline.

Juky, up front, was gibbering, "Oh, no, Massa,
please don't hurt me, I do whatever you say." He
spoke in a thick accent and dialect that, especially now
that Samson knew him, bothered Daniel Samson more

than anything else at the moment. They had to make
it look good for the witnesses, and this was how the
witnesses would expect a black man to act. He compared that with the real Juky he knew, and felt a wash
of shame at everything.

They snarled orders at Juky, struck him harmlessly
across the back a couple of times, and finally said,
"You bring that cart along with us now, nigger."

Contrary to what he had been told, they left him his
pistol. Baker's cousin must have decided to trust him
quite a bit. Samson knew it was childish and foolish of
him, but he stood for a long couple of minutes and
watched as the trap, surrounded by the riders, went on
up Harrison Street and disappeared around a corner.

He knew it might be the last he saw of Caroline or
Juky, and somehow he felt more alone than ever.

He turned toward the darkest street he could see,
figuring to weave his way in and out of the dark streets
and alleys of Manchester, so that it would not be obvious in which direction he was leaving the city. The
stench of the dirt of the alleyway invaded his nose—he
suspected chamber pots were dumped out of the windows above regularly—and the only sound was the
slight scrape his boots made on the packed earth, since
he was going quickly rather than quietly.

The man who jumped Samson from behind was no
professional as far as Samson was concerned. If Samson had had any friends within earshot, he'd have had
plenty of time to shout for help before the man got a
hand across Samson's mouth. And the grip the guy
took on Samson's right arm was too loose, so Sam-

son twisted out easily and kicked his assailant hard in the stomach. As he bent forward, clutching his guts, Samson whipped out his knife from his coat pocket and drove it forward and down with all his strength.

It was a lucky stroke. In the dark Samson had been aiming to drive the blade under the rib cage for the kidney, not to hammer it into the ribs themselves, but although he happened to hit too high, he hit between the ribs, and with the force he had used, the blade tore through his attacker's heart. As Samson wrenched the blade free and whirled to another corner in case any-one else was closing in, the man fell dead.

There seemed to be no one else, but he wasn't about to advance farther up the alley to find out. He started back the way he had come, found a dark enough side street, and stalked down it. Wherever that man had come from, he seemed to be operating alone.

He had wound through two more dark blocks, and was in sight of the Chesterfield Railroad, a little spur line that ran out to the coalfields south of the city. With luck, there'd be a train he could catch south. It would get him a lot closer to federal lines, especially if his memories were accurate and the Chesterfield area was slated for a cavalry raid within the next week. The railroad had a wide bend in it just south of Manchester, where he ought to be able to get onto a coal car and thus ride out unobserved.

He had walked only one more block when a quiet voice spoke behind him. "Lieutenant Heller, I believe your turn back onto Hull Street, toward the Mayo Bridge, was two blocks back."

Daniel Samson froze. He knew what that tone and the direction implied: he must be covered by several guns from several angles.

"Captain Maury," he said, "You are more than welcome to question me, sir."

"Why, thank you, Lieutenant. I intend to. Would you mind raising your hands and keeping them up? I assume you are able to perceive that you are standing in a shaft of moonlight, and therefore you can be seen much better than you can see, which is to say it will be easier for us to shoot you than for you to shoot us. Is that clear?"

"Very." Samson kept his arms raised and relaxed and deliberately didn't think about escaping. If he tried anything right now, with the caliber of agents who were probably surrounding him, he would be dead. He would have to wait and hope something would turn up, as unlikely as that seemed.

Hands touched him from behind then, gently because that was the way they were most likely to find what they were looking for, and checked him thoroughly. As they did it, Captain Maury commented, "We might have taken you earlier, you know, at the moment when you didn't turn back toward Richmond, but we let you finish off one of the more unpleasant criminals in the area first. Of all the men you've killed, he might have been the only deserving one, you murdering bastard."

When he had been searched completely—and this was a good job, they didn't miss a weapon—Maury said, "All right, then, spar him."

Samson's heart sank. His odds of getting away were dropping rapidly toward zero. "Sparring" was the method used to control the most dangerous and intractable prisoners, and he knew of no one who had ever been able to escape while sparred. In fact, he couldn't even imagine a way of doing so.

Yet by now, listening carefully to sounds of breathing and of shifting feet, he had identified at least six men in addition to the ones who had searched him. He was too outnumbered to fight or struggle, since the only thing that would accomplish was to anger them even more, so he relaxed and decided to face whatever was coming with as calm a mind as he could manage.

Always a good tactic, Master Xi said in his mind, but that was all the advice he got from that quarter, and he got none from any other.

Prescott Heller did drop in a brief request that if possible it would be better to be executed anonymously than to have word sent to his family. Samson shrugged mentally and agreed that, if it were up to him, he would get hanged or shot in the back of the neck without its being recorded.

They pressed his hands down behind his back, then bent his arms at the elbows and pulled his elbows back and his wrists forward. The wrists were handcuffed together with short cuffs. A seven-foot pole—the spar—was thrust between his elbows and his back, forcing a painful arch into his back and throwing him badly off balance. On a ring at each end of the spar, they attached a leg iron on a long chain. The leg irons were then clamped to his ankles, so that it was impossible for him to bring his feet together, and he had to stand in a slight straddle. Now he could only take short careful steps without flinging himself face-first onto the ground.

"All right, back to Richmond. March!" Maury's voice was cold, and there was no apparent interest in Samson now that he was sparred. The men around him moved without paying much attention to him.

There was nothing else to do but follow orders and hope for the best. He thought the worst would be the time he would have, walking a couple of miles with these baby steps, to think over everything that had gone badly, but he was wrong. Within twenty steps, the pain in his lower back and the backs of his upper thighs was so severe that he could think of nothing else.

Afterward, he vaguely remembered having fallen on his face three times, and the agony of being lifted back to his feet by four men grabbing the spar and raising him off the ground by it. The lights on the Mayo Bridge were very bright, he remembered, and he had a vague impression that the sentinels stared at him in astonishment, and that perhaps someone had looked at him with pity and been turned away by one of Maury's men, but the impressions were vague and shadowy, not much different from the nightmares he was to have after reaching his destination.

He had thought they would be going back to the Submarine Battery Service, or perhaps to one of the places where more secret work—such as torturing prisoners—was done, but instead they took him back to Castle Thunder.

The paperwork was simple and primitive, so that it was done in a minute or two, and then they took the spar off him so that they could march him upstairs.

"I must inform General Alexander that he's won his bet," Maury said. "I thought we would have to drag him here or throw him in a wagon, by the end of the bridge at the latest. You really are a fine specimen of manhood, Prescott Heller."

Samson heard but had no reaction to the words. As they released him, he discovered that about half of the muscles he needed to hold himself upright had been cramped for so long that he had no control of them, and he plunged to the floor, bruising his hands and face. They kicked him a few times, and oddly it seemed to help, perhaps forcing some muscles to loosen, so that at last he got to his feet and climbed the long, painful flight of stairs, gasping with dizziness and near blackout the whole time.

As a new prisoner, he didn't yet have a regular place to sleep. All the good places along the wall were taken up, and most of the straw that remained after that had been swept into piles around the pillars where the rest of the men slept.

"If you need to piss, follow your nose over to the open tile pipe in the corner," the guard told him. "You can crap in the bucket beside it. We catch you crapping in the pipe and we give you such a beating you'll be pissing blood for the rest of your life."

Samson staggered over to a stone bench that was near the latrine corner. There were two men on the top, wrapped around each other for warmth since they were sleeping on stone covered only by a thin blanket, and men stuck out in several directions from the stone legs, their heads propped up so as to avoid bugs in the mouth or nose and to get themselves partly out of contact with the floor. He found one part of one leg big enough for his head and, squatting down carefully, managed to lie down on the floor with his head against it.

In the middle of his first nightmare, he must have been screaming, because someone punched him in the solar plexus, not terribly hard, but enough to leave him woozy and confused. After that he dreamed on the cold stone floor, but what he dreamed, he didn't remember afterward, nor did he ever wish to.

7

By the time he woke up, someone had stolen his day's ration. It wasn't as though he was going to be in any mood to eat, anyway, and he was just as glad to miss out on the boiled corn, half a turnip, tablespoon of greens, with two tablespoons of bacon fat that one of the men told him it had been. The man also seemed very interested in urinating next to Samson, and he told Samson the whole set of rules for the prison, probably hoping to impress him, while Samson used the facilities, if that was the word for a tile pipe sticking out of the floor.

It was somewhere past noon, he realized. By now, if Juky and Caroline were going to escape, they'd done it, which meant he would hear nothing of them from now on.

He hoped he would hear nothing.

Castle Thunder was much less attractive inside than it was out, and much less attractive in the daytime than at night. The floor he was on was stone laid on timber, which had the interesting property of being as cold as a stone floor and as drafty as a wooden one. After having been sparred the night before, Samson woke on that floor with his muscles unbelievably stiff.

The other prisoners seemed to be amused at his twentieth-century stretching-out routine, as much as anything could amuse them. But they left him enough
space to do it in, which was generous of them considering that practically every available bit of floor was
taken up all the time.

As he pressed his forehead down to his knee and
stabbing agony shot up the underside of his leg, he
turned his head sideways to look around. Castle
Thunder was a pen for Confederates, not for Yankees, and a political prison rather than a criminal one,
so there were no uniforms there. Presumably the CSA
was broke enough to take a man's uniform back when
it caught him.

He spread his legs wide in front of him, put one fist
on top of the other between his legs, and pressed his
forehead down toward the upper fist. His legs felt as
though they were on fire from buttocks to toes, and
the small of his back felt as though he had just turned
it inside out. The odor in the place was unbelievable.
There were so many bodies never allowed to wash, a
single giant honeybucket dumped only every other
day, a lack of any water to flush out the "urinal," and
straw that probably hadn't been changed in weeks.
Mingled together, the odors made it hard to breathe.
Moreover, the temperature outside was rising rapidly
with the sun.

That particular day, he was not to find out what the
afternoon would be like in Castle Thunder. Two large,
quiet men from the Submarine Battery Service came
by, sparred him and signed him out. But they did the

sparring after he was taken down the stairs, and they placed him in the back of an old farm cart, with a canopy that kept him from the attentions of the crowds, so he decided that they weren't out to break him yet.

He found himself bound into a chair, seated across the table from Captain Matthew Maury, CSN. Maury stared at him for long seconds, and finally said, "All right, Heller, if that's your name, we have a mystery on our hands. If you really are Prescott Heller, I must extend my condolences. It would seem that a federal cavalry raid destroyed the Heller mansion, with the loss of your parents' lives, about ten days ago. Now, I would swear that you are the same man we sent north, but perhaps my memory is clouded or perhaps the man we sent north was not what he seemed to be.

"Or perhaps you have suffered a genuine change of heart. Unlike General Porter, I do not have any problem understanding that some Southerners might feel that the federal Union is somehow more important than the states that brought it into being. I suppose you might have been converted to Yankee views by living among Yankees.

"Or finally there is the possibility that the Carelias girl has brought about this change of heart in you. We have the testimony of two Negro servants at the Exchange Hotel as to where she spent the night, and I must tell you—" at this, Maury blushed slightly "—that, er, the proclivity of slaves for listening at the doors of their betters is as alive today as it was when Terence and Plautus were mocking it." The square-built man rested his hands on the table, pressing his fingers together in a little tent.

"Nothing you can say will convince us of your loyalty to our cause. Nothing will keep you from the noose when we are done with you. Understand that at once.

"We mean to know who you are really working for and what you are really doing. We don't know whether you will tell us, but we are willing to use physical persuasion. You can best stay alive by making sure we learn a few things we want to know every day. If we learn enough of them, you will suffer no pain on that day, either. The day will come when we execute you, but it need not come quickly.

"Now, General Alexander has suggested—and after some thought, I have concurred—that until you fully understand that you have something to dread, you will probably prove quite resistant. So without bothering with questions, but merely to teach you the implications of not answering them, I propose to make this afternoon quite uncomfortable for you. I have here Mr. Richard Turner, whose name you may know."

Samson knew it, all right, or rather Heller did. And although Heller had assumed that every report by Union officers returning from Libby Prison was Northern war propaganda, the man's reputation was such that Heller was as terrified as Samson. Richard Turner, inspector of Libby Prison, was so noted for brutality that several Northern states had already issued warrants for his arrest so that if and when he was captured he would not be allowed out of captivity before he could stand trial.

The small, glaring man who gripped Samson's lapels and shouted into his face would have been ludicrous if Daniel Samson had just had one hand free, but as it was, he was terrifying.

"We're going to buck you, boy, buck you all afternoon, and help you get thirsty!" the man shouted.

Maury, ever the gentleman, probably not wanting to know what was going to happen next, got up and left the room. The door closed behind him, and Samson found large men standing around him on all sides.

Master Xi, he thought, I am very afraid.

Of course you are. Keep whatever presence of mind you can, and resist wherever it is possible, and understand at the beginning that any man can be broken sooner or later, but most men can bear a few more seconds if they have to.

It wasn't particularly comforting advice.

When they grabbed him by his hair and pulled his head back, he was not ready for it and resisted more than he meant to. They hit him, twice, hard, with the backs of their hands, and Turner said, "Cooperate, Mr. Heller. Cooperation is the game we play here. You will learn to cooperate."

When they pressed on his jaw, he opened it.

The funnel they jabbed into his throat made him gag and choke, but when they began to pour something down it he was in real terror of being drowned right there in the chair. Whatever it was, he swallowed a lot of it.

"Common saltwater, Mr. Heller. I wouldn't have you fearing we had poisoned you." Flying into one of the fits of rage for which he was famous, he suddenly paced around screaming at Samson, slapping him with his gloves, calling him every name he could think of and demanding that Samson cease his insolence at once.

Realizing that if he spoke, he would be punished for that, Samson remained quiet.

Bucking was as simple and brutal a procedure as any ever devised. Samson had read about things like that being done by the death squads in Central America in his own time, and it had disgusted him to think there were human beings capable of dreaming up stuff like that.

They forced him into a sitting position and tied his arms over his knees, with a length of lead pipe over his arms and under his knees to keep him that way. Then they gagged him with a short length of dowel, picked him up, and carried him out onto a terrace in the sun.

It must have easily been eighty degrees when the process started, and the temperature climbed for the rest of the afternoon. At intervals that he couldn't figure out, they would come out and slap him to see if he winced. Apparently a couple of times he didn't, because he woke up as buckets of water were poured over him, leaving him more miserable than ever; with his mouth bound he was unable to get any of it into his scorched and burning throat.

His mind wandered back and forth, and memories from far back worked their way up into his con-

sciousness now and then: flashes of marching with
Caesar, with Henry, with Hengist, on wars of con-
quest, and flashes of dying at Cannae and Blenheim.
Somewhere in the far abstract part of his mind he discovered that he still knew how to field strip an M-16,
load and fire a Brown Bess and execute the basic short
sword drills with both *gladius* and *machaira*. He had
stood in the front rank of the phalanx for Alexander
the Great, and shot arrows into enemy phalanxes for
Judah the Hammer, stood his ground at Thermopylae and run like hell at Megiddo.

Pain, fear, thirst—these, finally, were not strangers. He knew that when they let him go today, he
would do anything to avoid going through this again,
but he also knew that he could if he had to.

The afternoon went on. It might have gotten hot-
ter. His muscles undoubtedly cramped more. He
found himself thinking that at least, after the dose of
salt, he wouldn't suffer muscle weakness from so-
dium loss. Now and then an ant or some small insect
would wander up his gritty, sweat-drenched shin or
calf, bent on exploring. He could do nothing to stop
them.

He kept his eyes closed after a while. The glare was
harsh and he would just as soon not see any more of
this particular terrace, anyway.

His memories of his past lives drifted away until
there was just himself.

And himself might be—Daniel Samson? Prescott
Heller? How would he even begin to tell the difference?

He felt Heller's grief at the loss of his parents, and his rage at them for not having been better parents, and his burning need for vengeance on the Yankees. He understood—and he wasn't sure whether it was Samson or Heller understanding—that what was happening to him wasn't necessarily any worse than what had been happening for many years on many plantations, that whether you called it "property rights" or "necessary authority" or "effective measures," no human being had a right to do this to any other.

And he felt that it was hot, and he was thirsty, and his muscles screamed with pain constantly, and his throat was too dry even to think about moaning.

It went on.

When they finally released him, the sudden pain of his muscles moving to different positions was so sharp that he fainted.

HE HAD vague notions of being shaken or slapped awake and forced to drink a good deal of water, but he didn't really revive till he was back on the floor of Castle Thunder. He sat up with a groan, realized what his first and most urgent need was, and hobbled like an invalid—all the stretching out of the morning completely undone—over to the open pipe. He urinated in what seemed like buckets, forever, feeling a sore cramping around his bladder when he was done.

Another man, emaciated, blond gray, with washed-out blue eyes, had come up to use it, and he leaned over next to Samson. "Who worked you over?"

"Turner."

The man's eyes got big. "How long till they, uh, do you?"

Samson hadn't heard the expression before, but it could only mean one thing. "I hang as soon as they get everything they want out of me. Or decide they can't get it. Won't be long."

"Wait a minute here, will you," the man said, and as he angled his urine against the side of the pipe to make a noisy, guttering sound, he whispered, "You're big. After what they did to you, can you still do something that's hard physical work if you have to?"

"I think so. Depends on what it is."

"What's your name?"

"Heller."

"Mine's Jarret. When I holler your name you come over and play along, if you want." He finished urinating and turned away. "Shit. Guard watching. Don't take this personal." And he kissed Daniel Samson lightly on the ear. "I won't call you for anything like that."

"You two there, stop that!" the guard shouted. Trying to look guilty, and noticing that Jarret seemed to be much better at it, Samson returned to his place on the floor.

Half an hour later Jarret suddenly bellowed, "Hey, Heller, over here and settle a bet for us."

He got up and ambled over, carefully stepping around the many bodies sprawled on the floor, picking his way because it was dusk and getting dark, because he didn't want to slip on the many damp spots on the floor, and most of all because he didn't want to seem too eager. While he made his way over to the group of men, he tried to look as puzzled as he felt. The guards seemed to have very little interest in the whole thing, which Samson was sure was part of the plan.

They were gathered around a stone bench identical to the one Samson had used as a pillow the night before. There were eight men, and they seemed—or was it just his imagination?—a little more nervous than a prison game to while away time could account for.

"You're the only guy as big as Big Luther, the guard that we saw pick up this bench and move it. Now what we've been arguing about is which is really harder, picking it up like he did in one clean grab, or setting it down like he did, real gentle because stone is brittle, so that even men standing right next to it said they didn't hear it make a sound. We don't have any idea which is harder because none of us can do either. But we thought, maybe you could, uh . . ."

"For a cut of the pot of course," one of the men added casually. "We could let him have one of the chunks of corn bread. There's five of those chunks and either way there's only going to be four winners at most. Save us problems dividing it up."

Samson still wasn't hungry—the torture and the stench of Castle Thunder had destroyed his interest in food or much else—but he strongly suspected that that had very little to do with what was really going on. "Sure, I'll give it a try. Now, I'm supposed to pick it up, all at once, one clean lift, you say?"

"Yep," Jarret said. "And then set it down, oh, say three feet over that way, making no noise at all, which means you've got to keep your grip and set it down gentle."

"I understand," Samson said. For the guards' benefit, he made a production out of the event, checking to make sure there were no damp spots he could slip on and no obstacles in his way. He spit on his hands and rubbed it in, though he had no idea why that would help in lifting a stone bench, stretched ostentatiously a couple of times, and finally squatted and lifted the bench.

It was very heavy, but not impossible by any means. In peacetime there were probably several men in the room big enough to do it, but most of them had been starved and prevented from exercise for so long that now none of them was in any condition to lift the bench. Samson stepped carefully backward, putting his feet where he had planned—that part had not been faked, you really could get hurt slipping with something this size in your arms—and then squatted slowly, using his legs and not his back with anything this heavy, going down slowly, waiting for the moment when he first felt the bottom of the bench touch the floor, then slowly withdrawing his upward pressure in a long slow breath so that the bench settled firmly onto the floor.

"Well, so which is harder?" one of them said.

"Got to be the lift, your veins practically popped out of your arms when you did that—"

"Naw, did you see his face when he was setting it down—"

There was an extensive argument about it, with the others shouting at each other while Samson stood there, scratching his head, trying to figure out what his role was next.

Jarret came to the rescue again. "Now, wait, wait, wait. Hold right on here. The man had never done it before. Naturally he doesn't have any idea, because his mind was all on whether or not he could do it and do it right. Now that he knows how, he can move it once or twice more and get a real idea."

Everyone nodded as if this were a profound thought, and Jarret turned back to him. "Heller, if you wouldn't mind doing it again..."

"Why, no, I don't mind a bit. Gets some of the knots out of my arms and back," Samson said.

He set himself carefully, braced, lifted the bench in one clean stroke, brought it up to where he could carry it, took the five steps he needed and again set it down without jarring it.

Okay, at least he knew one thing. Whatever it was Jarret wanted him to do, he needed to know that Samson could do it reliably. Which probably didn't mean doing a whole lot of it, but doing it once and getting it exactly right.

"Two more tries," Samson said. "Then I'll have an opinion." He wasn't sure, but he had a strange impression that this was really helping to straighten out his kinked muscles, anyway. Then again, after the afternoon, almost anything was bound to feel better.

Again he lifted it cleanly, moved it, set it down soundlessly. And again.

It was back in its original place. He had no idea whether that was important or not, but since Jarret had more or less given him the opportunity to get it back after the first move, it might be. Besides, he really didn't feel like hoisting it around anymore.

"Okay, I think I got it," he said. "It's hard work to pick it up, all right—" one group of them cheered "—but as long as you have a dry, clean floor to brace on and some solid place to hang on to, you're fine, and then it's just a big heave. Now, moving it is more of a job than you all are giving it credit for being." As he said that, there were groans from all of them, apparently at the thought that he might award it to neither side.

"But as long as you can just place your feet exactly where you're planning to," he continued, "that's no big deal either, just a matter of keeping that grip, so I suppose it would be pretty tough if you were holding on to a sharp edge or something." If what they wanted was similar to this, he certainly wanted that understood. "Now as for setting it down—" the other group cheered "—hmm. That's really tough. Got to be able to take your time, got to have a perfect place to stand, need to be able to bring it down real easy... yeah, I'd have to say setting it down without making any noise is definitely the hardest."

There were groans and cheers among them, and someone handed him a chunk of corn bread. "I'd eat that right now if I were you," Jarret said. "You're new here and you don't have any good hiding places yet, so if it doesn't go into you right now odds are it'll go into someone else. And a growing boy like you—" he looked at him emphatically "—really needs to keep his strength up."

Samson nodded and ate it. Naturally it was dry, and he suspected he might have ingested a bit of mold in the gathering gloom, but it was surprisingly pleasant to have something in his stomach.

"Gonna close up soon," the floor boss hollered. "No lights tonight, so get where you're going to sleep."

Samson turned to head back toward the urine pipe that was his major landmark in Castle Thunder, but Jarret took his hand. "I don't figure you left anything back where you sleep. And if you did, I'd reckon it must be gone by now. We've got some space in our little group, and it can help a lot to have other men around you that can watch out for you. Why don't you join us? All you had was a pillow spot over there, right?"

A pillow spot, Samson had figured out, was any small hard surface to lean your head up against. The other kinds were the much-coveted wall spot, and the completely despised floor spot reserved for prisoners who had made themselves so obnoxious to the other prisoners as not to be trusted near them while they slept.

"Yeah, a pillow spot on the side of a bench."

"Well, we have a pillow spot you can use. Leg of an old iron stove, shaped pretty well to fit your head up against. Wouldn't be any good in the wintertime, of course, but then I guess, from what you told me, that's an awful long time away for you.''

"Figure you're right. And I'd like a safer spot to sleep," Samson said.

"I'm going to get a little more air before I turn in. I see a spot at a window opening up," one of the other men said.

"You do that, Rodney. Bring back a couple bags of air for the rest of us."

From the halfhearted chuckles, it seemed likely that the joke was as stale as the air.

"Hey, Jarret! You leave that young boy alone!" The guard didn't seem pleased.

Jarret dropped Samson's hand. Samson by now had figured out that this was one of the most common ways to cover conversations you didn't want the guard to hear, since the guard would expect you to whisper. So as they walked back to the stove, he put an arm on Jarret's back for just a moment. "I know it's nothing, just a cover, to you," Jarret said, "but *I* am very likely to take it personally. That's how I ended up in here, and the guards know it. Part of the reason it works as a cover for me—but don't tease me, because I can't stand that just now."

Oh, well, Samson thought, dropping the arm, if Jarret had more to say to him, no doubt he would find a way. He also had to admit that it came as a surprise in this setting, but as they said back in the century he was from, some of your best friends probably were...

The corner of the stove really was more comfortable as a pillow, and Samson thought he might sleep a little better tonight because of that. Just as he was drifting off, Rodney returned from the window and said, "One. Go." He spoke the words as casually as you'd say "good night" or "where's my blanket?"

If "go" meant what he hoped it did, Samson would need all the rest he could get first. He yawned, stretched out and let himself drift. He was asleep almost instantly.

ONE HAND RESTED lightly on his mouth before another one touched him. There was a strange scraping noise that sounded like an enormous brass-plated snake crawling backward through a drain pipe. "Sit up," a voice breathed in his ear. "Don't talk."

As soon as he sat up, and his head was no longer in contact with the stove, the scraping noise disappeared. It was too dark for him to see, but he could feel bodies around him, crouched around the stove, and he could hear them working.

They were removing the bolts that attached the stove to the wooden insets in the floor, and doing it without making any noise. As he focused his attention, the voice added, "Now don't move. People have to pass close to you."

As the bodies went past and Samson held still, they became visible to him whenever they were silhouetted against the faint light from the distant windows.

They were carrying off every detachable part of the stove, including a large pipe that was clearly intended to feed into an even larger chimney.

Now that he knew what the plan was, Samson's heart was hammering. He couldn't imagine what the other men were feeling, after months in here as opposed to his scant day.

At last, after what seemed like a century of time, the voice whispered, "Crawl back to the stove."

Samson did, making no noise, and got to his feet. Two different people took his right and left hands and guided them to handholds, good, secure ones that Samson suspected they had cleaned and dried with their shirts in the dark. The voice whispered once more. "Straight up, gently. Back up seven of your steps. You've got a margin of safety behind you, but go *straight* back. Then set it down and come around it—don't bump it. Someone will guide you from there. Repeat that back."

Samson breathed softly into the ear that pressed against his. "Straight up, straight back seven, down gently, sneak back to this side."

"Do it."

Samson drew a deep breath silently and got prepared to expel it without any sound. Just from the feel of it, he knew the stove was considerably heavier than the bench, his hands were farther apart than they had been and thus his balance would be worse. Also he would have to carry it farther. He faced the difficulties, relaxed and, as he began his exhale, he lifted the stove.

It was heavier even than he had imagined, but he kept his balance, let his left foot extend behind him, settled weight onto it, and drew the huge, awkward thing between his arms back with him. *One.* Now the right foot, also as gently as he could, shift the weight completely first, pick it up, extend it back, place it...shift... *Two.*

He repeated the procedure five more times in the eerie quiet, hearing nothing but the breathing of the men around him, the sleepers farther away and the awake ones close to him.

Now set it down gently, which was quite a project.

He visualized the stove drifting down more slowly than a soap bubble, kept his grip firm, let his knees bend a little at a time, wondered if his upper thighs would give them away by loudly ripping his pants. He came down more, and more, resisting the little urge that chattered to him that his arms hurt very badly and that perhaps he was going so slowly that he had failed to notice when he'd made contact with the floor.

Down more, and farther, keeping it slow...he felt one leg touch, and let it sink until one by one they were all down. Slowly he gave the stove back its weight, and it settled onto the floor without a sound.

He was around it in a few more heartbeats, and a hand caught his sleeve. ''Forward a few. We've got a chimney open. You'll have to get down it with your back to the wall and your legs to the other side.''

''Right,'' Samson said. It was a normal rock-climbing maneuver, so he found that the only hard part was to move from one darkness into a darkness with nothing under him.

As he continued down, he heard a voice whispering up. ''Keep going till you touch bottom.''

He had thought they would be emerging on the first floor, but they must be going past because he could feel the little breath of air from where a stove was leaking a little around its seals, or perhaps the damper had been left open. Must be about halfway, he thought, and wished he'd counted steps coming down.

After another dark eternity, he felt his rump settle into a heap of ashes and very cautiously got his feet under him. A hand reached out to him and pulled him along. As he crept forward, keeping his head as low as he could, he suddenly found light.

They had come out in an unused part of the factory that appeared to be the place where air was heated to dry the tobacco. There was plenty of room now to stand upright, and light was pouring in from the street into the windows. A large furnace had been dragged out of the way.

Samson had to ask, so keeping to his softest whisper, he said, "Who?" and pointed at the furnace.

"Friends. Tell you soon," Jarret breathed back.

The rest of the party gradually assembled, and then another shadow moved in the basement. In short order, the new shadow had led them to a hole in the wall.

It was a tunnel, a simple dirt tunnel under the street, and thus under the dead line. It was a tight squeeze a couple of times for Samson, but he got through; he sure as hell wasn't planing to go back, anyway. All he had to do was occasionally expel his breath and force himself along, keeping his nose close to the butt of the man in front of him.

Finally, in the cellar of a saloon—at least judging from the beer smell—they came out. Before they did anything else, Jarret took a count and established that everyone who was supposed to get out had made it.

"Should we close anything back up?" someone asked.

"No," Jarret said. "Might be someone will find it before the guards, and the guards'll be in an uproar soon as they know we're gone. So it won't help the guards, and it might be it gets someone else out. What's the next stop on the journey?"

"Up these stairs. Soon as you all get up there we can have some light. Wouldn't do to have light showing facing Castle Thunder." There was something familiar about that voice, but Samson wasn't quite sure what it was.

They went up the stairs quietly, or as quietly as they could when several of them were so giddy that they were practically giggling. From the front of the saloon, they went into three large Conestogas, rushing quickly across from the front door to the wagons, avoiding being in the glare of the streetlights for more than scant seconds.

Inside the Conestogas there were dozens of wooden kegs, and the same thought crossed the minds of the men at once, for smothered chuckling could be heard everywhere. It wasn't as popular as it would be in future wars, but beer was still beer and soldiers were soldiers, and the idea of escaping in wagon loads of beer somehow added to the pleasure.

The drivers geed up the teams, and they were on their way. In a few minutes they were rolling down toward the river.

There were tense moments at the sentry posts, but apparently they were waved through. Then there was the rumble of the bridge under the iron wheels, and another wave through by a sentry, after one of them stopped to talk with the driver ahead of the wagon Samson was in; apparently it was nothing more than passing the time between men who had seen each other a lot.

They passed through Manchester in complete silence, and then through the opening in the Interior Line, and finally they came to a wide bend in the road and the guiding voice spoke again. "These wagons make this delivery of beer from Richmond to Petersburg every other day. But not two days from now, because the drivers are going north on the Railroad." Everyone seemed to feel like cheering, but they stifled it.

"Now, there's a couple of you that have people meeting you up here, and you'll be getting out with light in your face so if anyone up there recognizes you and wants you, you can go with them. But for most of you it's going to be up to you to get out. There's been Union cavalry raiding on this side of the river, but I have no idea where they are just at the moment. You all know the federals have landed on Bermuda Hundred, so I reckon if you walk that far you're bound to find what you need."

Samson had finally realized whose voice it was, and his heart wanted to leap up and sing. But he waited until it was his turn to climb down from the wagon, and then took a slow look around. The light in his eyes didn't allow him to see people.

Maybe Juky had decided that he didn't trust Samson, and would just let him go up the road on his own, or even send someone after him....

"Over here, Toole or whatever your name is," he said. Samson walked into the dark, and his friend's arms flew around him.

"I'll be damned. I'll be double damned. How'd you end up in there? Thought you had a clean getaway."

"So did I. Way it goes." Samson hugged back.

He could feel Prescott Heller recoiling from the touch of black flesh, and he sent a flash of fury at him. For once Heller didn't retaliate, but instead reacted with puzzlement, wondering how could anyone fail to notice what Juky was.

What he is, Samson thought, is brave and decent and smart. How can *you* fail to notice that?

No answer came back, and he was glad of that.

"Just ran into bad luck. Did you all get away all right?"

"Almost." Juky sighed. "Old Mr. Carelias... well, he wasn't very strong. Next afternoon in the woods, on the way south, he just up and died. Miss Carelias didn't take that too well. Getting Daddy out has been the main thing in her life for two years now."

"How is she?"

"She'll be all right pretty soon, I'm sure. With all the fighting, we've been having trouble with getting anybody over the Potomac, so she's holed up at Ma's. I was headed there with the drivers from these wagons. You can see her tonight."

Samson gave off an odd little laugh, the only sound that he could get out past the great lump of joy clogging his heart. Juky clasped his arm again, and this time even Prescott Heller made no complaint.

8

They took trails toward Ma's that wound around far from the roads, and as long as they stopped to listen frequently, it was safe enough to talk.

Juky's story was straightforward enough, though like anyone in this field, he had run severe dangers several times. They had gotten out of the city successfully, and behind them, in the dark alleys of Manchester and along the lonely roads south, more than a hundred armed men, black members of the Railroad side by side with white members of the Peace Society, had closed in to kill the detectives that Alexander and Maury had put on their trail. "Most amazing trip I've ever had in eight years on the Underground Railroad, Sean. You don't mind if I keep calling you that?"

"Any name you want to call me, Juky, I'll answer to it."

"Well, the one order they gave us was not to look back no matter what—afraid that one of them might get the idea about what was going on. Made me feel like Lot in the Bible. See, if they'd bagged the first couple of detectives, the ones following us most closely, the rest would have known, and they'd have been a lot more careful in following us, and most likely they'd have given some of our men a much bigger fight than they did. As it was, far as we can tell, we got every one of them. Twenty-two of them dead to just three men wounded among us. All but a couple of them taken cleanly from behind."

The Virginia woods on a spring night were alive with birds and animals. Samson had never been hiking here in the twentieth century, but he doubted very much that it could have stayed this wild. There was a whole feast of the sounds of insects, birds and frogs, and the smells were wonderful, as well...damp mud and mints in the creek bottoms, hardwood and thick grass higher up, sand and pine now and then.

And he would be seeing Caroline soon.

Just the same, he was interested enough to want to hear the rest of the story from Juky, and since they had some miles to go, he listened to the rest between pauses when they had to cross roads and stop to listen for patrols....

They had gone on for miles, hearing nothing behind them, until the last mile of the night's journey, when they had begun to slow down as they approached the preselected campsite. If the plan was working properly, this should cause the surviving detectives to bunch up behind them and thus to fall into an ambush, trapped from behind by the ones who had been following them and in front by an armed group of more than thirty men.

There had been just six detectives left by then. It was as if the carriage had slowly rolled out of Richmond, strewing corpses in its wake. The six detectives had arranged themselves into two groups of three, one on each side of the road, and waited nervously for more men to show up, while the Peace Society and Railroad fighters, knives drawn, had crept toward them in dead silence.

When they finally struck, the detectives in one group had been crouched in the brush in a vehement argument that was abruptly cut off as three throats were slit at once. The other party had just time to jump up from where they had been lying, and to draw pistols, when suddenly they stopped more than a dozen throwing knives in midflight.

Juky had been able to creep back to get in on the kill, and he couldn't conceal his satisfaction. "Sean, I saw men dead who I know have sent back a hundred slaves and hanged a dozen Railroad people. It was the biggest blow we've ever struck, and the best. It will take them years to get back to closing down Peace Society and Railroad safe houses and making arrests at the rate they were. Slaves will be *pouring* north for months, especially now that there's an Emancipation Proclamation. And even though they don't have the leaders they had, I bet you the Peace Society is going to take some ground and hold it."

Samson was a little surprised to hear that that was important to Juky, but his friend chuckled. "You have to realize, nobody knows white Southerners like we do. If they come out of this war thinking they were a united country that got its ass thrashed, in fifty years the grandkids of people who fought and died on the Railroad and in the Peace Society will be singing Dixie and flying the Stars and Bars from their porches. It's the same thing as the ancient traditions they talk about that are only twenty years old. All you have to do is get one year past living memory and you've got people believing whatever you want. But if Alabama or Georgia takes itself right out of the war and rejoins the Union—well, then that'll be different. The decent folks that never kept slaves and never held with keeping 'em will have, uh . . ."

"Committed themselves," Samson said, but he felt sad, because he knew that it was what Juky feared and not what he hoped for that was going to happen. Since he couldn't tell him, he would have to let his friend find it out for himself.

The morning after that night of knives, Telemachus Carelias had gotten up very weak and raving, and despite being given nourishing food and plenty of attention, before noon he had become unconscious, dying shortly after. They had marked and recorded the place where they buried him, and Caroline—very nearly in shock, from what Juky was describing—had gone to Ma's, partly to recover and partly to wait for Juky to have a party headed north she could join. "She'll be all right, Sean. Honest she will, I promise. The problem is that her whole life went into rescuing her pa, and then just when it looked like she had . . . well, you saw what he was like. But even then he could at least have lived his life out in comfort if she'd been able to get him home and nurse him back to health, and that didn't happen, either. She put two years of her life into that rescue and it was really for nothing, far as she can see. Maybe later she'll be able to see that our getting rid of so many of the detectives and rolling up so much of their organization was a very large gain, and that she and her father were vital to the operation. But right now she's just hurting with so much of her life and heart and courage being thrown away like that.''

Samson sighed, a long, soft sigh, thinking to himself that he might spend years comforting her.

If he had years. He was still in a war zone, he was still wanted dead by at least one side, and he was still Daniel Samson, who attracted trouble the way a carcass attracted flies.

Then there was the problem that he didn't know whether he had made his life right in this time. Prescott Heller was a better being than he had been. Surely, if nothing else did, heartbreaks would make a youth grow into a man. Also, Heller had come to see the world in a somewhat broader perspective.

Somehow Jackson Houston had died as a genuine hero, after a lifetime as a low-life petty hood. Hiram Galt had gone down fighting after a long, difficult fight for justice, one that had strained his every resource to the breaking point.

So far, Prescott Heller was a little wiser and a lot sadder. What was it that was missing?

For the last mile or so, Juky insisted on silence. "Lot of federal patrols have been out."

"They're on our side, aren't they?"

"I wish I was sure," Juky said grimly. "Don't forget there are plenty of Northerners that hate us colored men, too, and plenty who only wanted this to be a war to save the Union. Cavalry raiders aren't too particular. They know their job is to destroy things, and they know that they'll seldom get in trouble for anything they do. They may not care whose side anyone's on. It's just better if they don't find any trace of us."

The idea seemed very cynical to Daniel Samson, but then he let his memories roam back to the other wars he had been to. He had known men in Vietnam who made no distinction between North and South and who did things—or at least bragged about doing things—while out on patrol that turned Samson's stomach to hear about. He had given testimony at one court-martial where an American corporal had savagely raped a little girl in front of her mother, and the father had been a sergeant in ARVN, the *South* Vietnamese army at the time. With a shudder, Samson remembered that the only thing the corporal had said during the whole trial, over and over, was "They are Viet-muh-nese, and we are here to fight them, ain't we?" Even as he was being sentenced, he still seemed not to understand why or what was wrong with what he had done.

At least in his home time, it had been possible to try someone for abusing civilians. His memory of the First D.C. Cavalry and of cavalry raider units he'd known was that nobody in them ever expected to have to stand trial for anything, unless perhaps the war was lost.

Well, Ma's place was well hidden, but he'd be glad when he got there, and gladder still when they were back in Washington, D.C. Caroline would feel better with rest and quiet for a while, and—

And Dan Samson was bound to be dead soon. He had been in World War II for four days, and in the Mexican War for less than three weeks. He had been here for five or six days. There was no way he could imagine that he would have time to do more than see Caroline one or two more times, and to make as sure as he could that she would be all right.

The weight of all the past lives to be straightened out, stretching in front of him as far as his mind could conceive, seemed like a mile of anchor chain fastened around his neck.

Master Xi clucked at him. *Now you yourself have figured out that your destinies are interlocked. You will see each other many more times.*

But, Samson thought, I don't *want* to have a lot of short visits in every period of history. Especially because we could just as easily meet in lifetimes where I was nineteen when she was eighty, or vice versa. I want to meet her again in a way that will fix what was wrong.

My screwed-up life cost me my marriage. And now I find out it was this long string of past lives that screwed up my life. I want them all unscrewed up, and then I want to go back and get things right with Sarah. Or Caroline. Or whatever her True Name is—what the hell is a True Name, anyway?

The world seemed to shimmer around him, as if the whole solid earth, the trees and creeks and rivers, roads and bridges and armies on every side of him were just a veil drawn over something much more important and wonderful. *You have thought of the right question, or the first right question!* Master Xi exclaimed. *Very few of us would have thought you could possibly do that for many lifetimes yet. You may be much closer to what you want than you—*

Juky grabbed Samson's arm. "Some kind of trouble up ahead." He turned to the three runaways who had been quietly going along with them, and said, "You men stay here, and stay here with your knives drawn. Not getting stabbed is up to Sean and me, and you give anything that comes this way a fight until you see it's a friend."

They nodded solemnly. Juky went to his belly and wriggled forward to where little glints of light were playing through the leaves, and Samson followed. As he crept forward behind Juky, his hands almost on Juky's boots, he smelled smoke.

When they were lying side by side under an elderberry bush, they found themselves looking down at the last flickers of the fire that had consumed a little wooden shack. Six people were sitting dejectedly in the yard, knees drawn up to their chins.

"Do you know this place?" Samson asked in a whisper.

"Free Negro family," Juky said. "Not real respectable folks . . . We never really trusted them enough to try to get them into the Railroad, not with a good station like Ma's so close. Could be they just had a fire, but I don't think so. Guess we have to go down and ask, but I'm dreading what we're going to hear."

"Do you suppose that Ma's place—?"

"I don't know, friend, I just don't know. Could be these people here just had a fire. And even if it was paddy rollers or cavalry raiders or something, this place you can see from the road, and Ma is well back. She's most likely fine. But we have to ask these folks, I think. Let's go."

Samson felt a little ashamed of himself. What Juky had said was only common sense, and Samson had only Caroline at Ma's, but Juky had many friends and comrades of many years' standing. And whoever might have done this, if it wasn't just a fire, had come through here hours ago from the look of that fire and by now they'd either missed Ma's place or been and gone.

Juky walked up to them cautiously. It took Samson, following after, a moment to notice that there was something odd here, and then to realize what it was. The two boys were in trousers and shirts, but the woman and her three girls were naked.

And all of them were sobbing.

Juky squatted down. The weeping woman looked up at him but didn't meet his eye. "What happened? Where's Amos?" he asked.

She pointed toward the smoldering remains of the shack. "They shoot him and leave him lay. Amos move but they don't let us drag him. He burn up in there."

A mask of fury slid across Juky's face, as sudden and as deadly as the rearing of a cobra. "Who did this? Who?"

She sniffled and shook her head.

"Hepzah, I will believe you. I will believe you no matter who you say did this." The killing fury hadn't left Juky's face. "But I have to know. You have to tell me."

The older boy, who could not have been much more than ten, said, "Linkum riders."

Juky and Samson swore. *Lincoln riders.*

Union calvary.

"Can we send you help? Can we get you to a friend's house?" Juky asked. In the dying red glow of the house, Samson could see a tear streaking down his face.

"They hurt—" Hepzah couldn't stop weeping. "Down here," she said, pointing to her own crotch. "They take sticks burning and they burn me and my girls."

"They beat me, Mama, I couldn't stop them, they had me tied up—" The oldest boy was sobbing, the helpless despair of a child who had found himself powerless and felt himself—as all children do—to be to blame.

Samson could feel cold icy hate forming down in his bowels, as well, and he knew that whatever Juky wanted to do about this, Samson would be right with him.

"Cover yourself," Juky whispered, "cover yourself and your girls." He turned to the older son. "You and him find some cloth or clothes, maybe you had some stuff on the line, so your mama and your sisters can get dressed. If you don't find anything else, us men will give them our shirts. Come on, they need you to do this."

The boy got up, with no light or hope in his eyes. But he had a purpose now, and he set about accomplishing it.

Juky turned to Samson. "Go get the drivers. We have to move now. Bring 'em down here."

"Yes, sir." Samson shot up the hill to where the drivers crouched, announcing himself firmly to avoid getting stabbed. As he brought them down the hill, he met the older boy coming back from the spring house with some laundry that had apparently been soaking in tubs there. Awkwardly he put an arm on the boy's shoulder and said, "Nothing and no one could have saved your mother and sisters. You did the best you could. You were very brave to try to fight at all."

The boy shoved Samson's arm off.

Way to go, be an idiot, hurt the kid worse, Samson thought, just before the boy shyly reached out and took his hand. They walked together like that down to the shack.

Juky was all business. He put it to them simply as Hepzah and her daughters got dressed in the bushes. This family needed some help or it would starve. The drivers were to stay here for two days, get some kind of shelter built for them, and get the tiny farm back to functioning just as quickly as possible. If anyone white turned up on the road, the drivers were to go into the woods and stay there until it was safe. At the end of two days, the drivers were to come to Ma's by a route that he carefully coached them on.

The three men nodded, and Samson was sure they'd do it, but he could see the horror and rage that burned in them.

Uncle Sam's cavalry was really out there winning him friends, he thought. He knew there were atrocities in all wars, and that American soldiers were soldiers like other soldiers...but he couldn't make himself feel philosophical about it. This was certainly worse than anything he'd seen personally in Nam, and this was done by American soldiers to American civilians on the same side.

Normally Samson hated killing. He was good at it, but he wasn't the sort of man who could ever learn to enjoy it or to treat it neutrally. Just now he felt an overwhelming need to kill somebody, somewhere, right away.

Juky turned to him. "That's taken care of, as much as we can do. Which, Christ in heaven, isn't much. You wearing boots you can run in? Reckon I could do the two miles without being useless when I got there. Can you?"

Daniel Samson nodded. "You lead, friend. I'll be right with you."

The forest that had seemed so friendly and pleasant before was now a place of nightmares. Shadows formed crouching ambushes, trees seemed to reach for them like claws, every rustle of a deer or a rabbit was someone dying in the brush. The air that had smelled clean and fresh was poisonous and thick. Samson ran through it with his heart freezing inside him, knowing that whatever he found might well be worse than whatever he could imagine.

Ahead of him, Juky ran on tirelessly. The man was made of iron. It was only his presence, Samson thought, that had held them together so many times on this mission, and right now he was having to depend on his friend's common sense, for rage and fear had left him nearly incompetent. He half prayed for a fight in the forest, uneven as the odds would be, because Juky's revolver and Samson's knife would be up against the Union cavalry's eight-shot Spencer repeating carbine. He didn't care. Anything to work out his terror and fury, to eliminate his terrible doubts.

The trail they were on broke onto the moonlit wagon track that would lead to Ma's place, and they gained speed as the ground became clearer.

There was just a moment for Samson to think before they came around the bend that the track was almost invisible from the road, and most likely they had military targets to attack, as well, so they probably rode right on by.

But then they had made it around the bend, where the ground was softer, and saw the trampled ground. Many horses had gone through here...in both directions.

The cavalry had been here and left already. They had done whatever they had done. There was nothing Samson, Juky or anybody could do now.

Juky gave a wild cry of despair that echoed how Samson felt. Samson's eyes were so full of tears that he could barely see to run.

They didn't slow down. Rather, they picked up the pace of their running. At least Ma's house wasn't on fire, for there was no trace of flame or smoke. Someone there might still be alive, however badly hurt, or perhaps they had all successfully hidden from them in the cellar....

Samson's breath was coming in ragged gasps. He knew how dangerous it might be to arrive out of breath, and he didn't care. He ran as hard as he could, and yet Juky was almost gaining ground ahead of him.

When they finally rounded the bend to Ma's place, there was no need to speculate any more. Ma and three of her regular workers had been hanged from trees in the front yard.

Juky went to his knees on the ground and beat it with his fists, wailing in anger and frustration. Samson stood and stared.

Someone had nailed a signboard to the tree:

    Hey Reb
    We Kilt Yor Slavs
    No Mor Nigers 4 U
    Union 4 Ever

Ma's body swayed slowly and turned in the slight breeze. The hands that had tended so many children, cooked so many meals, done so much work that needed doing, and the legs that had carried her hundreds of miles, seeing people to freedom and then returning herself when she might at any time have stayed North and safe herself, hung uselessly from her. The fearless voice and the heart that had driven it were stilled forever.

Samson sank slowly to the ground next to Juky, sitting there in silence next to his brokenhearted friend. He didn't want to know any more than he knew already.

Juky sighed and finally said, "I can tell you something now."

Samson said "What is it?" with no curiosity at all.

Juky didn't seem to notice Samson's uninterested tone. "I know everyone else called her Ma because she made herself everyone's mother whenever she could. But... well, she *was* my mother."

Samson was startled. He realized it was Prescott Heller's shock registering within him. "But you were born a slave, Juky. How could a free Negro be your mother?"

"Because she wasn't free. She was a runaway. I was trying to get her out of the South—it was one of my first trips as a conductor for the Railroad. But Ma, well, I never did win any arguments with that woman." Juky gave a little snorting half laugh and tears surged down his face. "When she understood what the Railroad did, there was nothing for it but she had to work in it. Couldn't talk her out of it. God knows I tried. She wouldn't even do any of the work up North. She...she knew this could happen, and she took her chances, and my mother was certainly a grown woman...but oh God, I'm going to miss her."

Samson put an arm around his friend and let him sob. They sat there for a long minute or two before Juky said, "You know we've been here a while and Caroline hasn't come out."

"Uh-huh."

"So if she didn't get away, then, uh..."

"She's probably in the house, dead," Samson said. It wasn't that he couldn't feel it. Rather, it was that he felt so much just now that there was no way to express any of it. He stood up and shook the dirt off himself because somehow the idea of tracking dirt into Ma's house was something he just couldn't imagine doing. "Can you come with me? I don't want to go in by myself."

Juky nodded, and they went in side by side.

They didn't have to look for her. She was dead on the big dining table in the kitchen. She was tied to the table, arms over her head, legs spread wide, and her throat had been slit. Most of her clothing had been cut away.

Juky grabbed a tablecloth from the laundry basket still sitting absurdly on a little table to the side and threw it over her. Samson turned it back just enough to see her face and tenderly closed her eyes and kissed her on the lips. It had crossed his mind for one moment that they might have missed the major blood vessels, that perhaps she was just in shock...but no, her face was cold and quite stiff, and her eyes had dried so that there was no gleam or sparkle in them.

"I can…arrange her," he said to Juky. "If you need help tending to your mother—"

"Just a hand getting her and my brothers down. I couldn't bear to just drop them."

They got a ladder from behind the house, and in a few minutes the job was accomplished. The four bodies were lowered as gently as two strong men could manage, and the ropes cut from their throats.

Samson left Juky to attend to his kin, and went back up into the house to cut Caroline out of her bindings and compose her body. Rigor mortis, just now setting in, made the job painfully difficult, because he hated to apply force to her delicate little frame, but he did it.

It was only after he finished that he saw the note staked to the wall with a jackknife. He struck a match, lit a sputtering tallow candle and held the note up to the light to read it.

There were a couple of pages, and two different handwritings. The first was done with careful precision, but was made of big round loops and whorls, the sort of writing you might get from your girlfriend in high school.

Dearest, beloved Daniel,

    Absurd as it is, they say they are going to claim me as a prisoner of war and take me back to the Union encampment at Bermuda Hundred, along with Ma and her sons. They have poor Ma scuttling about like a panicked hen, trying to get her valuables into one heap so that she can take her ''wealth'' with her. I don't suppose it amounts to more than fifty dollars worth of things in all.

But here I am going on like a girl with all the time in the world to write, and what I must say is only that as soon as I am transported North I shall seek out Cousin Lafayette and that neither I nor he will have any rest until you are completely exonerated. You will be able to find me encamped in his lobby, arguing on your behalf, or if you don't return until I've won the case, then most assuredly he will know where to find me. Daniel, I believe—I always will believe—everything you tell me, and so I know without asking that you will find me wherever I am. And I remain your most steadfa— Oh God, Daniel, they have taken all of Ma's stuff when she brought it out. They are getting out ropes and there are men at all the doors here. I cannot hope to run they say they will let me finish this letter maybe two of them look ashamed, the rest Daniel I am afraid of what I see in their eyes. Daniel I love you. I will always love you we will find each other no matter what you promised I promised And I Love You....

Your Caroline

Daniel Samson tried very hard to stop reading right here. He had as much willpower and self-control as anyone alive, but there are things that even ten years of experience with *ninjutsu* don't make possible, and so his eyes registered the heavy, childish printing that took up the rest of the page, the big, black capitals burning into his brain, and his mind couldn't help but develop them into the words.

Hey Reb
Hey Daniel The Reb
We All Did Her & It Was Good
She Beggin For Mor So Mutch We Had 2
Kilt Her 2 Git Sum Rest
She Is A Good Hoar But Beg 2 Mutch
& 2 Many Nigers Did Her All Redy
Ha Ha Ha Ha

Very, very carefully, so as not to disturb one line that Caroline had written, he tore the foul words from the bottom of her letter. He put her letter into the inside of his shirt, next to his heart, then took the ugly fragment and burned it in the candle flame till there was nothing left and the burning paper singed his fingers.

But though he could burn the paper, he couldn't burn the words. They would be with him for a thousand and more lifetimes, he knew. And his heart would hurt more than his fingers did. Nothing could hurt more than his heart.

He bent to uncover her face and kiss her once again. He needed to say to her something like what he had said to the boy back at the shack, that some things couldn't be helped, that good people must not blame themselves, that nothing they had done to her could change his love for her. To his surprise, he realized the impulse came not just from himself, but from Prescott Heller, and he realized, as well, that there was a big difference there.

Samson had learned, from Sarah and from others, that rape wasn't the victim's fault, that the blame must always and only fall on the rapist. It was a commonplace in the 1990s, where he had come from. But in Prescott's day, if a man's fiancée was raped, the man angrily shoved her out the door. Prescott Heller had been brought up with the idea that the victim was always to blame. Yet he had made that leap—how? From picking through Samson's memories? From some innate decency surfacing?

From love. It was that simple. It was one thing they both shared: they had loved Caroline, deeply and completely, and if Samson's love had had the added force of another lifetime behind it, Heller's had had the passion of first love.

And when he looked down into her face—knowing that after he said this, he wouldn't look again—he didn't say it, for the cold flesh on the table was no longer Caroline.

Samson hadn't gone to church in decades, except to see friends married or buried, but when he was a teenager he'd gone regularly to please his mother. He remembered now the part of the story that always got into the Easter sermon, that when the women came to Jesus's tomb on the third day after the crucifixion to anoint the body, the angel had asked them who they sought. They had said "Jesus of Nazareth." And the angel's answer had been "he is not here."

As Samson looked at Caroline's body, he realized that that was true of everyone, and true of Caroline now; she wasn't there. She was, perhaps, in the Wind Between Time, on her way to some other life, or even now being born somewhere else in the world. He knew she hadn't crossed over from the Wind, because he had known her as Sarah, but he couldn't imagine that she had anything like the heavy debt to work off that Samson did.

He pulled the cover back over her face and whispered, not to the dead flesh, but to the living spirit wherever it was, "I'm coming for you."

Out on the porch he saw that Juky had finished laying out his family and was standing over them quietly, head down, probably praying. He bowed his own head in respect, but instead of praying he found that he had a lot of thinking to do and a lot of feelings to sort out.

Prescott Heller was very active in his mind just now. And the thoughts that came from Heller made a certain terrible sense, something Samson might not have acknowledged even a few minutes ago.

Heller loved his home. The same sort of men who had done this had burned his home and killed his parents. Many things in the South were dear to Prescott Heller's heart, and if the Yankees succeeded, their cavalry would tear through to do this. By picking through Samson's memories, he had already learned, to his deep horror, what Sherman was going to do to Georgia and what Sheridan would do to the Shenandoah Valley.

There was humility in Heller now, too. He could admit that slavery had been wrong, that the race hatred he had grown up with had not been good for either himself or anyone else. He could even admire the courage and dedication of Juky and be glad to have had him as a friend.

But there was absolutely no escaping the fact that if agents like Juky succeeded in their missions, if the Union armies did well, then horrors and atrocities of the kind he had seen here would be unleashed on the South. Not everywhere and not by everyone—many Union soldiers would be downright chivalrous—but still the hapless Southern civilian population would be turned over to men with guns who could do whatever they wanted. Some men, in that situation, were lower than any animal was capable of being.

In fact, Heller reminded Samson, it wasn't until Lincoln had decided to keep the Union together by warfare—which is to say, decided to let this sort of thing loose—that Virginia, North Carolina, Arkansas and Tennessee had seceded. They had been willing enough to remain if their fellow Southerners hadn't been threatened with...with the sort of thing that they were witness to.

Samson wanted to have some answer for Heller, and he had none, not right now, not maybe for a long time.

It was, after all, the North, and Abraham Lincoln, who had decided that the Union must be preserved, even at the cost of bloodshed—that the Union must be preserved, and not that the slaves must be freed, a goal which had only been added recently. Many good and decent Southern men were in the field to protect their homes because, in their judgment, the other side had "cried havoc and let slip the dogs of war." And many Northern troops, fighting for booty and a chance to run loose on an undefended population, were morally no better than the most brutal overseer.

Samson had no resolution for it. To his credit, neither did Heller. But Prescott Heller wouldn't feel ashamed if he fought to preserve his homeland from destruction, and Daniel Samson wouldn't be able to condemn him.

Juky finished his prayers and said, "I know you're tired, but I have to do something. I won't be able to sleep. I'm going to dig some graves."

"I'll help," Samson said, and as the sun came up, it found them hard at work with shovels. Samson's back ached intensely from all that it had been called upon to do and to endure, but he didn't manage to care about it much. Pain was good. If there was enough of it, he didn't think.

9

They were still digging a half an hour after the sun had come up, and they had made at least one concession to the physical world; they had a tin pitcher full of water, and a cup, on a rock between them. Ma had owned more than one cup, and Samson, raised on twentieth-century ideas of sanitation and propriety, had been about to get one for each of them when Prescott Heller had pointed out to him emphatically that Juky would read that as a deep, wounding insult, so he had quietly gotten just one.

They were finishing the last grave when they heard the distant hoofbeats. There was a sizable force, more than one company, moving south along the Old Stage Road, but whether it was Confederate or Union was impossible to tell at the distance. They shrugged to each other and went on digging. Temporarily they were both out of the war, with more important things to do.

But when they both got back into it, Samson's mind whispered to him, what then? Would he be on the same side as Juky, a man with whom he would gladly stage a two-man commando raid on hell? Or would he defend the homeland he loved?

It was exactly that kind of thought he had been in the process of avoiding, so, cowardly or not, he pitched in with more of a will to get the grave finished.

Then there was a thunder of hoofbeats, someone riding fast and hard, coming up the wagon track to Ma's place.

"Shit," both men said, and then smiled at each other.

"Juky," Samson said, "my suggestion is that you get down into the priest hole and stay there, because this force is going to be too big for us to fight, and a white man stands a better chance of being someone they'll listen to. Hell, I might even get some help with the burials. Now don't be a hero—go hide."

Juky had been about to object, but there was just enough common sense in it that he sprinted into the house, closing the door behind him.

Samson kept digging. He wasn't going to put himself into a situation in which he might have to volunteer any information, regardless of who showed up.

From the sound of it, they'd be here in a minute or so. They were certainly riding hard enough.

The sky was such a deep blue it seemed odd that he couldn't see the stars, and the whole earth seemed to be bursting with life today. He had never heard so many birds in his life. He wondered if that was something as simple as the lack of motor traffic, which even at its softest was always so much louder than the murmuring of the James River, not far away. Even the freshly broken earth smelled good, and he found himself thinking that he might take time this afternoon to pick flowers for Caroline's grave.

It seemed terribly wrong to feel that way.

The hooves were now very loud.

Nonsense, Master Xi said. *You aren't wrong to enjoy whatever life you can find. Caroline will not be happier for your suffering, nor will Juky's family. A day of picking flowers, and of reflection, would be a good thing for you, Daniel Samson, if you only had the time.*

Do I? Samson wondered for a moment, and then the Confederate cavalry troop galloped up.

One glance told him what was about to happen. It was the same troop they had met on the road before. They hadn't seen Samson that time, but no doubt they'd been given plenty of description, and the fact that they were here meant they knew what the place was.

He tried to play innocent, and began to climb out of the grave. He was doing his best to catch Dr. Roger's eye to see if he could get any help from that quarter.

They reined in and sat there looking at him, as if they didn't quite believe it.

Their captain glared at him and said, "Gentlemen, I do believe this is the man we've been looking for for some days, and from the holes he is digging, I would say that blue-belly we captured was telling the truth and they already did most of our work for us."

"Not the kind of work they did," Samson said. He tasted the clear air of this fine morning, and decided he could leave any time, as long as he didn't betray

Juky while doing it. "You'll see inside. I know what's going to happen to me, so don't put me in one of those . . . they're for the others. And I know you have to look to see who they are, but you'd be better off not seeing what the Yankees did to them."

The captain stared at him for a long, hard second, and said, "This is some trick."

"No, sir." Samson, hands over his head, walked slowly toward the captain. "By now you must have it down in your orders—I know Captain Maury and he's very thorough—that I've escaped too many times, and they don't want you to bring me in. Am I right?"

The captain seemed a bit taken aback, but he nodded slowly.

"I'd rather not hang. I've been near to a hanging a couple of times and I'd rather die like a soldier, which I am, even if I'm out of uniform. It's a small favor, and really, less work than putting up a noose."

The captain appeared to be considering it when Dr. Rogers winked at Samson and gestured, with his hands held close to his body, for Samson to drop his hands.

Daniel Samson had been betrayed many times, and been kept faith with many times, and he had no idea which was happening, but he liked Rogers and preferred to trust him. He dropped his hands suddenly, and a fusillade of pistol shots, badly aimed from haste, tore into him. He felt his body shred behind him, and he fell over backward.

In a moment Rogers was bending over him on one side, and the captain on the other. He felt the needle go into his arm and knew what the doctor was up to... and approved. Between the wounds and the morphine he had just been slipped, he would be dead before he could betray anyone.

The Wind Between Time was beginning to howl. Samson hoped Juky would be all right, but he seemed to have a date to keep— "Captain," he heard a distant voice saying, "there's two shovels here. There might be another man somewheres."

Samson was almost out of reach of the world, and he could tell that he was too weak to speak... but he felt his vocal chords form a sound. "Captain," Prescott Heller was managing to say. "Listen to me—"

No! Samson shrieked, but he was half over into the Wind already, and he no longer had control. In a moment, in the hope of striking even one small blow for the South, and even having grown to respect Juky as he had, Prescott Heller would reveal where the black Union agent was hiding. And Samson couldn't hope to prevent it.

He tried to fasten a grip on Heller's mind, and he felt it slipping....

At that moment he felt other grips coming to his aid. Jackson Houston and Hiram Galt, the other personalities he had redeemed on previous trips, were coming in on his side. For a time that was probably one long breath for the captain and Rogers, but which seemed like hours to Samson, the struggle seesawed back and forth.

He visualized it a thousand ways. Hiram Galt tracking Prescott Heller through a high pass in the Rockies. Jackson Houston face-to-face with Heller, knives extended at each other's bellies, circling and circling in the tough streets where Houston had grown up. A squad of Houstons in American uniforms slugging it out on an Italian hillside with a squad of Hellers in German uniforms. Hiram Galt crouching in the chapparal, sighting in on Heller....

And then for one instant, they had him, and they held him, and they turned to Daniel Samson, and said, *Tell him.*

And not knowing quite what he was thinking, Samson let his thoughts wash outward over Prescott Heller, all of the memories he had from the civil-rights struggle that had been in its acute phase when Samson had been young. The days when any decent American overseas had had to feel a little twinge of shame because someone was bound to bring up segregation. A small, brave black girl, running the gauntlet of chanting racists, surrounded by the Stars and Stripes and the National Guard. Rosa Parks not giving up her seat on that bus. Martin Luther King, Jr., and the dream he voiced at the Lincoln Memorial. Freedom Riders, and buses in flames by the side of the highway, and the murders in Mississippi.

Southerners, Prescott. Freedom won by people from Birmingham and Montgomery, Selma and Atlanta, one group of Southerners demanding it from another—and getting it.

You tell them where Juky is, and after they hang him they won't even mark the grave.

You tell them where Juky is, and it's one more we all owe for.

Are you going to turn in a fellow Southerner?

The breath was bubbling in his throat, and he suspected more than one sucking chest wound, but he managed to say, "Put flowers on the girl's grave. Put flowers on her grave."

There was a great gust in the Wind Between Time, and all of them—Daniel Samson, and Jackson Houston, Hiram Galt and Prescott Heller—spun off into the Wind. In the great span of lives below, Samson saw the flickering gray stench floating around the life he had just left, then saw it dissolve and the clear sweet glow shining forth.

One more.

He hung in the Wind Between Time, where to think of a question is to know the answer, because there were things he truly needed to know, now.

IT WAS ALWAYS the same question at first when he came to the Wind Between Time . . . what would have happened without Daniel Samson's intervention in the past life?

The short answer was that everyone would have died then, too. At the first interception of the party, all but Samson and Caroline would have hanged, but when she realized who had betrayed them, she had pulled out her dueling pistol and shot Prescott Heller through the heart. Her next shot had bagged the sergeant. . . .

And the men had raped her in the ditch by the side of the road, and then beaten her to death with a shovel.

Telemachus Carelias had died in prison. Ma and her sons had perished at the hands of the same Union raider.

Booth had still gone on, alive and well, to his eventual date with a performance of *Our American Cousin* in the Ford Theater, an event that would be remembered for reasons that had little to do with acting. No power on this side could have stopped what was fated to be there.

Samson looked it over and acknowledged that some good had been won by his efforts, but his heart was still hollow and sad.

Normally it was not a place where there was time, but it seemed to him a very short while before he sensed Juky's presence. "They caught you anyway!"

"Yeah, they did," Juky said, in that way of talking that only happened in the Wind. "But you didn't help them. So, I'm on my way. Hope you find everyone you're looking for.... I'll see you when you make it to the other side."

And so quickly and cleanly that it barely seemed like motion, Juky had crossed to the other side of the Wind Between Time, that mysterious place where Samson couldn't go until he had solved the problem of all of his past lives. He knew that Turenne a.k.a. Bastida was trapped like he was, in this cycle of lives to be redeemed, and he sensed that Jim Strang a.k.a. Matt Perney and Sarah a.k.a. Caroline had passed this way not long ago, on the way to other lives.

Once I meet them a few more times, he thought, it will be pretty hard to think about them, what with all those names strung together....

Not if I learn their True Names.

Now he sensed what a True Name was, and most importantly, that to learn the True Names of the people to whom he was bound in this wandering through time was the first of the Five Keys, the things that, when he had them all, would allow him to return to the original life and to undo the crime he had committed, whatever that might be.

If he knew their True Names, he could find them when he needed them.... And then another thought struck him. The Union irregular who had raped and murdered Caroline, slaughtered Ma's family—didn't he have a True Name, too?

This is not a question you should ask yet, Master Xi said.

What? Samson asked incredulously. There's an order I'm supposed to earn these brownie points in, or something?

Do not mock what you don't understand. In time you will be ready to know other things—

But nothing stays concealed in the Wind Between Time.

Samson knew now that just as he himself wanted to undo his original crime, and might find a chance to do so, there were beings who drew their very existence from that crime, spirits of pure evil who returned to human life again and again, and that the one who had murdered Caroline had been one of those ancient foes of humanity.

So I created him? Samson thought, revulsion rolling through him.

But what he has made of himself since is in part his own choice, Master Xi said.

But I'm responsible for his existence. You can't deny that. And only I can get that stain out of the universe. The realization hit Samson like a hard punch, along with his first knowledge of what it was he truly had to do.

Very well, you know that much, but there is so much more you must learn before you can—

I want that sucker, Samson thought. I want him now.

You aren't ready. First you should learn how to use a friend's True Name—

Perhaps it was only because he had just come from being an adolescent. Perhaps he was still consumed by deep fury over what had happened to Caroline. Maybe he only wanted to know that he could defy Master Xi if the need arose. But whatever his real reasons, Daniel Samson had formed a question and demanded its answer in the Wind Between Time, and now he knew.

He knew that he had met three of his necessary companions, and he had two more to meet.

He now knew the first of the Five Keys, and thus knew how to ask what lifetime he could find it in.

And perhaps most importantly, he knew that there were three adversaries and that one of them had touched his life in that foul and brutal way.

This next trip is the payback for Caroline, he said. And for me.

He formulated one more question: when was the last time that the two companions he still had to find had clashed with the adversary who had raped and murdered Caroline?

He knew. And moreover, he knew that in that lifetime, he could find the First Key, if he were lucky.

No! I must absolutely forbid this! Master Xi, for the first time ever, seemed to be frantic. *You are not yet strong enough to fight a power of that kind, and you must not risk failing when you reach for the key, and in that lifetime winning your two companions to your side will be harder than it was at almost any other time.*

So it would be a tough job. Here in the Wind Between Time, Samson had no shoulders to shrug with, but he thought a shrug at Master Xi anyway. Danger was nothing new. Fear would always be there. High stakes made it interesting. Ahead of him there was an all but impossible job, a foe who might well prove too strong for him, and two friends as good as any he would ever have—if he could win their respect and love.

For Daniel Samson, that was plenty of reason. He focused on that life and shuddered. Even among all the rottenness of his past lives, this one was unusually foul and disfigured. It was also much farther into the past than he had been before.

Maxter Xi was still begging him not to do it as he felt himself drawn down toward that life.

Daniel Samson thought, Let's . . . go.

AFTERWORD

The Civil War is the most dangerous of all possible territory for an American writer doing any sort of historical fiction. This is not because too little is known, but because so much is; no war in our history, even in the twentieth century, has been so thoroughly documented by so many historians. Thus the first obligation after having written such a book is to apologize and say that undoubtedly many errors have crept in, and that sources that might have permitted greater accuracy have been overlooked.

With that much said, let me at least point out some choices I have made deliberately. Covert operations in the 1860s were conducted out of many different offices for many different purposes. Nothing corresponded to the centralized agencies we are familiar with today. The Union side is at least documented, though not very well: Lafayette Baker and his Secret Service were as real as I could make them. On the other hand, because there was good reason to fear criminal trials after the war, the Confederacy's secret agencies destroyed all the records they could, and most memoirs even after 1900 were circumspect about some aspects of what they did. The case for operations run out of the Submarine Battery Service and the Signal Corps, by Maury and Alexander, respectively, are quite solid. The speculation that Booth was a Confederate agent and that the Lincoln assassination was a covert operation that went awry is argued forcefully and well in Tidwell, Hall, and Gaddy's *Come Retribution,* but it's distinctly a minority view. For using it here I make no apologies; it's interesting, and works of fiction fundamentally are about what is interesting rather than about what can be documented.

The USS *Commodore Jones* did really hit a mine in the James River and sank on May 5, 1864, with the loss of all hands, though not quite where I've put it. There is no existing evidence that it was involved in any covert operation, but when Baker's agents were dropped into the South, it was frequently Navy gunboats that dropped them.

The subject most likely to give offense in this book, I suppose, is atrocities by both Union and Confederate troops. On these, I stand firm. Nothing has been described here that was not reported by credible witnesses, though I have freely changed locations and names. Union irregular cavalry raiders *did* severely abuse and often kill free blacks, partly due to racism that was hardly less common in the North than in the South, and partly because their job was random destruction and these were the people least able to fight back. Confederate prison authorities at very high levels *did* permit, and sometimes encourage, the torture of federal agents for information. Wars are brutal, civil wars are particularly brutal and covert and irregular operations are often brutal by design. I have chosen not to romanticize this.

Active and sometimes armed resistance to the Confederacy was very widespread, and it is not uncommon for Southerners documenting "Uncle Elmo who fought in the War" to discover to their chagrin that he fought on the Union side. Some of the cavalry units which scouted for Sherman during the Atlanta campaign, for example, were made up of men from northern Alabama. The image of a united and homogenous Dixie is chiefly a product of the twentieth century, of *Birth of a Nation* and *Gone with the Wind*. Reality, as it often is, was much more complex than the myth, and there is surely much for all Americans to be proud of in the courage and steadfastness of the now-forgotten Southern unionists.

The first of Daniel Samson's adventures was written in a time when my life was collapsing around me; elsewhere, I've thanked the many friends who got me through that time. As I write this, it is almost a year to the day later, and I have at least the beginnings of recovery underway in a new city. Old friends you can count on are part of life's miracles, but more amazing to me, looking back, are the people who befriended me and helped me get back on my feet in a town where I knew nobody and where I was too numb to have much to offer in return at first. It takes a very special person to come to the rescue of strangers. So I'd like to thank many people at the University of Pittsburgh, both students and faculty, but especially my fellow students in the Ph.D. program in theater arts, and most especially Sherry Caldwell, Gregg Dion, Beth Marecki, Mark Kittlaus, and Frazer Lively—very special people.

Back to the beginning . . .

PILGRIMAGE TO HELL $4.99
Out of the ruins of worldwide nuclear devastation emerged Deathlands, a world that conspired against survival. Ryan Cawdor and his roving band of post-holocaust survivors begin their quest for survival in a world gone mad.

RED HOLOCAUST $4.99
Ryan and his warriors must battle against roaming bands of survivors from Russia who are using Alaska as a staging ground for an impending invasion of America.

NEUTRON SOLSTICE $4.99
Deep in the heart of Dixie, Ryan and his companions come upon a small group of survivors who are striving to recreate life as it was once known.

CRATER LAKE $4.99
Near what was once the Pacific Northwest, Ryan's band discovers a beautiful valley untouched by the nuclear blast that changed the world forever.

HOMEWARD BOUND $4.99
Emerging from a gateway in the ruins of New York City, Ryan decides it is time to face his power-mad brother—and avenge the deaths of his father and older brother.

Here's your chance to find out how it all began!

Gold Eagle brings another fast-paced miniseries to the action adventure front!

by PATRICK F. ROGERS

Omega Force: the last—and deadliest—option

With capabilities unmatched by any other paramilitary organization in the world, Omega Force is a special ready-reaction anti-terrorist strike force composed of the best commandos and equipment the military has to offer.

In Book 1: **WAR MACHINE**, two dozen SCUDs have been smuggled into Libya by a secret Iraqi extremist group whose plan is to exact ruthless retribution in the Middle East. The President has no choice but to call in Omega Force—a swift and lethal way to avert World War III.

The year is 2030 and the world is in a state of political and territorial unrest. The Peacekeepers, an elite military force, will not negotiate for peace—they're ready to impose it with the ultimate in 21st-century weaponry.

WARKEEP 2030

by MICHAEL KASNER

Introducing the follow-up miniseries to the WARKEEP 2030 title published in November 1992.

In Book 1: **KILLING FIELDS,** the Peacekeepers join forces with spear-throwing Zulus as violence erupts in black-ruled South Africa—violence backed by money, fanaticism and four neutron bombs.

KILLING FIELDS, Book 1 of this three-volume miniseries, hits the retail stands in March, or order your copy now by sending your name, address, zip or postal code, along with a check or money order (please do not send cash) for $3.50, plus 75¢ postage and handling ($1.00 in Canada), payable to Gold Eagle Books, to:

In the U.S.	In Canada
Gold Eagle Books	Gold Eagle Books
3010 Walden Avenue	P.O. Box 609
P.O. Box 1325	Fort Erie, Ontario
Buffalo, NY 14269-1325	L2A 5X3

Please specify book title with your order.
Canadian residents add applicable federal and provincial taxes.

WK2